"Wait!"

Tyler halted in midstride.

Michelle scooped in some much-needed air before going on. Still, her voice came out breathless and husky. "I...I don't want you to go. I want you to stay."

He spun around slowly on his heels, his face wary. "Meaning what?"

"Meaning I...I want you to stay."

"All night, you mean?"

She hadn't really got that far in her mind. But once the thought was there, it made her head spin. "Yes," was all she could manage.

Dear Reader,

I admit it! I find playboys fascinating. I love reading about their glamorous lives, their beautiful women, their many affairs. There's something exciting about these wicked devils who dare to do what an ordinary man wouldn't—or couldn't.

I've always thought a playboy makes an excellent romantic hero, because he is the ultimate challenge. Can one special woman make an often cynical man reassess his lifestyle and yearn for something finer, deeper and more permanent?

When my editor asked me to write a trilogy, I happily chose playboys for my heroes. Three handsome Aussie males who seem to have it all but find, once they meet that one special woman, that they want *her*...her respect, her love. Only, this time getting what they want isn't so easy as it usually is.

I hope you enjoy AUSTRALIAN PLAYBOYS. Do write to Harlequin Presents® and let us know what you think—and which heroes personally appeal to you!

Miranda Lee

Miranda Lee

THE PLAYBOY'S PROPOSITION

The Australian Playboys

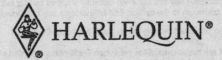

HARLEQUIN®

TORONTO • NEW YORK • LONDON
AMSTERDAM • PARIS • SYDNEY • HAMBURG
STOCKHOLM • ATHENS • TOKYO • MILAN • MADRID
PRAGUE • WARSAW • BUDAPEST • AUCKLAND

ISBN 0-373-12128-8

THE PLAYBOY'S PROPOSITION

First North American Publication 2000.

Copyright © 2000 by Miranda Lee.

CHAPTER ONE

MICHELE LEFT the office just after six, her colleagues' congratulations still ringing in her ears.

She'd been in a 'think-tank' all day, bouncing ideas back and forth for an advertising package the company she worked for was to present to a client mid-May, less than six weeks away.

Admittedly, some of her ideas had been pretty good. But she'd still nearly fallen off her chair when, at the end of the session, the boss had chosen *her* to head the Wild Ideas team. But by the time she'd ridden the lift to the ground floor and left the building, shock had given way to a tiny whisper of trepidation.

Because Wild Ideas hadn't actually won the account yet. They had to compete against another as yet unknown advertising agency for the lucrative job of revamping Packard Foods' Single-Serve meal line.

Michele walked slowly up the city street, reassuring herself that she was more than ready for this challenge. She was twenty-eight, with five years' experience in advertising; a lifetime in that game! Some confidence restored, she glanced up, too late to avoid bumping into the back of a woman waiting at the kerbside for the lights to change.

'I'm so sorry!' Michele exclaimed, embarrassed.

When the blonde turned round, Michele flashed her a sheepish smile. 'Sorry, Lucille. Wool-gathering.'

Lucille lived in the same apartment block as Michele. She had, in fact, been the real estate agent who'd sold Michele her unit.

But Lucille had moved on from property sales this past year to work as a relocation consultant, making life stress-free for company executives being moved to Sydney from either interstate or overseas.

It sounded a glamorous job, and it paid well, too, if Lucille's clothes were anything to go by.

Coolly beautiful and always turned out to perfection, Lucille could probably have had her pick of men. But she'd been burned by marriage to the biggest male chauvinist pig of all time—according to Lucille. Since her divorce had been finalised several months earlier, she'd been going through a 'I hate all men stage'.

Michele suspected this wouldn't last for ever. Lucille was far too young at thirty to embrace celibacy indefinitely.

Michele had become quite friendly with her this past year, and they sometimes went out together for a meal, or a movie.

'Working late again, I see,' Lucille chided.

Michele glanced at her watch while hitching her handbag higher on her shoulder. It was ten after six.

'You ought to talk,' she countered. 'Madame Workaholic herself!'

Lucille shrugged. 'Working's better than sitting at home twiddling my thumbs and wishing for the moon.'

'The moon? Don't you mean a man? Admit it, Lucille, you don't really want to live all by yourself for ever.'

Lucille sighed. 'I suppose not. But I'm not interested in getting married again. I'm not interested in *any* man, either. I want a man who actually *likes* women. A man who has hot blood running through his veins, not cold beer. A man who will put me first, and not his mates, or his golf game, or his infernal car!'

Michele laughed. 'You're right, Lucille. You're wishing for the moon.'

The lights turned green and the two girls crossed the road together, then turned right for the short down-hill walk home.

Their building was named Northside Gardens, though Lord knows why. The only gardens to grace it were the flower boxes some occupants had put on their not-so-large balconies. Three storeys high, its outer architecture very fifties, it was a simple cream brick building with its six front steps shaped in a semicircle.

The interior, however, had been extensively renovated and modernised, with the bathrooms fully tiled and oak kitchens installed before the twelve apartments had been offered for sale the previous year.

They'd all been snapped up in no time. And why not? They were relatively inexpensive for the area—possibly due to the dated façade and lack of a harbour view. But their position right in the middle of North Sydney was second to none, especially if you worked there, as both Michele and Lucille did. It only took

Michele ten minutes to walk to work in the mornings. Seven, if she hurried.

Michele took longer walking home these days, perhaps because she wasn't as eager to get there as she was to get to work. She, too, was living alone at the moment. But she was expecting Kevin to beg her to take him back any day now. He invariably did. She just had to be patient.

'How come *you're* walking home today?' Michele asked as they stopped at the brick wall outside their building and collected the mail from the built-in letterboxes.

Lucille needed wheels for her job.

'Had a prang this afternoon,' Lucille replied. 'The car's been towed away for repairs.'

Michele was momentarily distracted by the ornate white envelope she'd just drawn out of her letterbox. The embossed picture of wedding bells in one corner suggested a wedding invitation. Who on earth amongst her friends and relatives could be getting married?

Lucille's bad news finally registered, and Michele glanced up quickly. 'How awful for you! Are you okay?'

'Fine. It wasn't my fault, either. Some fool in a sports car careered straight into the back of me. Driving too fast, of course. A bit like this dear chap coming down the street now.'

A gleaming black Jag roared down towards them, zapping into the kerb right outside their building, smack dab in a no-parking zone. The driver was out in a flash, slamming the car door behind him.

'Who the hell does he think he is?' Lucille snapped. 'Doesn't he think the road rules apply to him?'

'Probably not,' Michele said drily as her gaze raked over the man in question. 'That's my dear friend Tyler. Tyler Garrison. Remember? I told you all about him.'

Lucille's finely shaped brows lifted. 'So *that's* the infamous Tyler Garrison. Well, well, well...'

'Do you want to meet him?'

'No, thanks. I don't have much time for playboys, no matter how good-looking they are.'

Lucille disappeared in a flash, leaving Michele to watch Tyler make his way around the front of the shiny black girl-catcher.

There was no doubt he *was* good looking. *Too* good-looking.

Frankly, Tyler was too everything. Too handsome. Too smart. Too charming. But above all...too rich.

Her eyes travelled over his clothes as he strode purposefully towards the pavement—and her. The superb navy suit draping his tall, broad-shouldered body would have cost a mint. As would the Italian shoes and snazzy blue shirt. The gold-printed tie was undoubtedly silk, its colour the ideal complement for Tyler's bronzed skin and tawny blond hair.

All in all...perfection personified.

Michele conceded ruefully that during their ten-year acquaintance she had never seen Tyler look anything less than physically perfect.

Except once...

It had been back in their university days, during their last year. Tyler had been playing football with the college team and a rough tackle had sent him to hospital with his legs paralysed and suspected spinal injuries. Michele had gone to visit him as soon as she'd heard, sneaking in after visiting hours—only a possibility because he'd been in a plush private room in an expensive private hospital where the patients' wishes came first and super-specialists moved heaven and earth to restore their clients to health.

Michele had been shocked by Tyler's bruised and battered state. She'd been shocked by his mental state as well.

He'd put on a brave face with her for a while, but hadn't been able to keep it up after she'd taken one of his hands in hers and gently told him he'd still be a beautiful person even if he *was* paralysed. He'd actually cried in her arms that night…for a short while.

Michele almost laughed now at the memory, and the silly way it had affected her at the time. Still, she'd always been a sucker for lame ducks. But a girl *did* like to feel needed, she'd always found. And Tyler had needed her that night.

Thank heavens her disturbing feelings had only been a temporary state of affairs, as had Tyler's paralysis. His spinal cord had only been bruised and everything had been back to normal in no time.

Tyler certainly looked anything but a lame duck today. He looked exactly what he'd always been—the glorious golden-boy heir to a publishing fortune. That one brief episode had been a mere glitch in the perfect and privileged path Tyler was destined to travel.

'New car?' she remarked as he stepped onto the pavement in front of her.

'What? Oh, yes. Bought it last month.'

Michele smiled wryly up at him. Tyler traded in cars as often as he traded in girlfriends. 'Got bored with the Merc, did you?'

The fact he didn't smile back at her, as he usually did, quickly sunk in.

Michele's stomach did a flip-flop as she realised it was actually very odd for him to turn up on her doorstep like this. Odd for him to be looking so worried as well. Tyler never looked *really* worried. About anything!

Instant tension sent her fingers tightening around the envelope she was holding, crushing it within the palm of her left hand.

'What?' she burst out. 'What is it? What's wrong? Oh, my God, it's Kevin, isn't it? Something's happened to Kevin.' She grabbed Tyler's nearest arm, her heart racing madly. 'He's been in a car accident, hasn't he? He drives like a lunatic. Even worse than you. I'm always telling him to slow down or he'll—'

'Nothing bad has happened to Kevin,' Tyler broke in, taking her hand off his arm and enfolding it firmly within the two of his. 'But, yes, I *have* come to see you about him. I thought you might need me.'

'Need *you*?' she echoed blankly.

He smiled, a smile which looked strangely sad. Now Michele was truly thrown. Tyler looking worried *and* sad?

'Well, I *am* the last of our little group left to lend

a shoulder to cry on,' he drawled. 'Everyone else is overseas. Or married.

'Or about to be,' he added quietly.

Michele just stared at him for a long, long moment, a black pit having opened in her stomach. She was an intelligent girl. You didn't have to hit her over the head with a baseball bat to get a message across.

Finally, her eyes dropped to stare down at the wedding invitation she was still clutching. And crushing.

Now she knew who had sent it.

Kevin.

Kevin was getting married. But not to her, the girl who'd loved him since their first term at university together ten years before. Who'd been his steady girlfriend during those wonderful four years. Who'd been his live-in lover for another two years afterwards, and on and off ever since. And who'd been stupidly waiting since they parted the last time, at the beginning of the year, till he came to his senses and realised he would never find another female to love him as she loved him.

'My invitation was in the mail when I arrived home,' Tyler explained. 'I immediately thought about you coming home from work this evening—all alone—and possibly finding a similar one in your letterbox. So I came straight over.'

'How... brave of you,' she said in a strangled voice.

'Brave?' The corner of his mouth lifted in a wry fashion. 'I wouldn't say brave, exactly. But you were there for me when I really needed you. Something I've never forgotten. Let me return the favour now.'

Michele blinked up at him. How strange that he should mention that incident, right after she'd been thinking of it, too.

So he *hadn't* forgotten their brief moment of emotional bonding. Odd. She rather wished he had.

'Who's he marrying?' she asked tautly, not wanting to look for herself. 'Do I know her?'

'You've met her. At my New Year's Eve party. Her name's Danni. Danni Baker.'

Michele felt sick to her stomach. Kevin had broken up with her for the last time shortly after that New Year's Eve party. Now she knew why.

Anger swept in to replace her stricken distress. 'So I have *you* to thank for this, do I?' she flung at Tyler, tearing her hand out of his sympathetic grasp.

Tyler reeled back momentarily from the bitter accusation. 'That's hardly fair, Michele.'

'Maybe not, but it's true!' she wailed. 'If you hadn't kept inviting us to your fancy parties! If you hadn't impressed Kevin so much with your impossibly luxurious lifestyle, making him crave more money than he could ever earn! If you'd just stayed out of our lives!' She sucked in an unsteady breath, which escaped again as a sob. 'Now he's going to marry some beautiful rich bitch whom I could never compete with in a million years.'

'I'm sorry you feel like that, Michele,' Tyler said stiffly. 'I happen to think you could compete with any woman. You have brains as well as beauty.'

Michele had no patience with his flattery. 'Oh, come now. Brains? Since when did a man value brains in a wife? As for beauty; I know what I look like. I'm a passably attractive brunette with a passably attractive figure. End of story.'

'I think that's understating things. You're a *very* attractive brunette with a *very* attractive figure. Okay, so Danni's a stunner. I admit that. And, yes, she's rich. But she's not a bitch. Frankly, I feel sorry for her. You and I both know Kevin's not marrying her for love.'

'I certainly do, because Kevin loves *me*!'

'Does he now?' Tyler's tone was brutally caustic.

'Yes!' she insisted, even while reality was dishing up a different story. If Kevin loved her, why was he marrying someone else?

And then to have the insensitivity to send her an invitation without even telling her! My God, she'd had coffee with him less than a month ago and he hadn't said a word about any involvement with Danni. All he'd talked about was work. Kevin was in advertising as well. He'd been having some trouble making up a jingle for a new account. She'd given him a few ideas and he'd called her an angel for helping him.

The dismaying realisation that he'd merely been picking her much lauded brain that day sent tears welling up into her eyes.

'The only person Kevin loves these days,' Tyler snapped, 'is himself. Come on, don't start crying in the street. You know how you hate making a show of yourself in public. Let's get you inside. And then you can have a good cry in private.' His hand gripped her elbow and he began to steer her forcefully up the front steps.

Michele felt considerable irritation at this take-charge attitude, which was perverse. He was only being kind. But in truth Tyler had always had the ability to irritate her, right from the first day they'd met at university, when he'd breezed into the lecture room looking like something out of *The Great Gatsby* rather than a genuine student.

When all the other girls' eyes had widened at first sight of him, she'd just rolled her own and turned her attention to Kevin, who had been cute and charming, plus a real student, genuinely passionate about the course they'd just started. Kevin had *needed* his degree in graphic design and visual communication to get on in life, whereas Tyler had needed nothing but his birth certificate.

Despite Tyler's brilliant results during the next four years, Michele had always felt he was just amusing himself at university, passing the time till he was old enough for his father to put him in charge of a section of the family's empire. Tyler had already completed a business degree before moving on to their course, which explained why he was four years older than most of them. If it had been up to her she'd never have let him join the little group they'd quickly formed, but when they'd needed a sixth for a video assignment Kevin had asked Tyler, and their so-called friendship had started.

Michele wasn't sure exactly what Tyler saw in his five less privileged friends, or why, over the years, he'd refused to let them simply drift away, as so often happened with student-day friendships. All five were regularly invited to his many and varied parties, although all five didn't always attend these days. Linda certainly hadn't, since moving to New York to work on the *Times* two years ago. Neither did Greta, now that she was married with a baby and living back in her hometown of Orange. Jeff turned up occasionally, but even he was spending more and more time in San Francisco since finally admitting he was gay.

The only reason Michele went was because Kevin always dragged her along. But she really didn't like the feelings Tyler evoked in her. Around him, she was inclined to become a real shrew, such as now!

'You'll have to move your car first,' she told him tartly as he steered her towards the glass security doors 'or you'll get a parking fine.'

'Forget the damned car. You're more important than some silly parking fine.'

'Spoken like a true millionaire!'

Tyler ground to a halt and glared down at her. 'What is it with you and my money? I can't help being born rich, any more than Kevin could help being born poor!'

'No, but you can certainly help wasting your money. And throwing it around like it has no value. We mere working-class mortals have to worry about such things as parking fines, you know.'

'I do know that, Michele,' he ground out. 'Very well, where can I park legally around here? Does this building have garages, or a guest parking area?'

'Yes.'

'Well where, for pity's sake? I can't see any drive-way.'

Michele looked up into Tyler's increasingly frustrated face and realised things were going to deteriorate from here, as they often did when she and Tyler found themselves alone together nowadays. The scenario was becoming depressingly familiar. Tyler would criticise her over her one-sided and ridiculously forgiving love for Kevin. Then she would make nasty cracks back about his endless parade of girlfriends. All those six feet tall big-boobed model types who dripped all over him and hung on his every word.

The truth was they came from different worlds and should have parted company years ago. They had nothing in common. Nothing whatsoever!

Michele sucked in a deep steadying breath, counted to ten then exhaled slowly. 'Look,' she said in her most reasonable voice. 'Why don't you just go home? I appreciate your thought in coming here to see how I was. But I'll be fine, I assure you. I certainly won't be going upstairs and throwing myself off the balcony.'

'I don't imagine you will,' he said drily, 'since you only live on the first floor.'

Michele frowned. 'How do you know I live on the first floor? You've never actually been up to my apartment. You've only dropped me off here the once, from what I recall.' Kevin had had too much to drink at Tyler's last Christmas party, and had passed out on the floor, whereupon Tyler had insisted on driving

Michele home. They'd argued about Kevin the whole way home.

Tyler shrugged. 'I sat outside in the car after you stormed off inside on that occasion, counting to a thousand. When a light came on the first floor, I assumed that was your place. After all, it was four in the morning and all the other windows were dark.'

'Oh…' Guilt and shame crawled like spiders in her stomach. She really had acted abominably that night. She wasn't doing much better now.

As much as she hated to admit it, Tyler had been quite a good friend to her over the last few years. Hadn't he often rung her at work and taken her out for coffee, or lunch, right when she'd needed someone to show they cared about her? Invariably he seemed to know when Kevin had gone off on one of his 'finding himself' jags.

Tyler was so right. He couldn't help being born rich, *and* beautiful, *and* brilliant. And she supposed he couldn't help being a bit of a playboy. What other man, in his position, wouldn't be the same?

But it irked her just the same.

'If you want me to go,' he said, rather tiredly, 'I'll go.'

Now she *really* felt ashamed. The least she could do was invite him up for a drink, or a cup of coffee.

After all, he had driven here *all* the way from Point Piper, she reminded herself, sarcasm creeping back in. A whole two miles or so!

Probably just wanted to take his flashy new car for a run through the harbour tunnel, came the added waspish thought. Or maybe his date for tonight lived over this way. Last time he'd taken her out for lunch he'd explained he just happened to be in the area, supervising a fashion photo shoot down at Balmoral Beach for the precious women's magazine Daddy had given him to run.

How typical that since Tyler had taken over its management it had become a raging success. He'd changed the name from its earlier innocuous title to *Rags to Riches*, then included some feature stories between the fashion pages which tapped into women's fantasies. Success stories mostly, and makeovers, not to mention endlessly superficial but perversely fascinating profiles of Australia's most glamorous females. All fodder for Tyler's little black book. No doubt he...

Michele closed her eyes. Dear heaven, she was doing it again!

'Michele?' Tyler said softly. 'Are you all right?'

She sighed and opened her eyes. 'Yes, Tyler, I'm all right. And, no, Tyler, I don't want you to go. Come on. I'll show you where to park and then we'll go upstairs for a drink, or coffee, or whatever.'

His eyes glittered as a wickedly sexy smile lit up his handsome face. 'I'm very fond of whatever.'

Michele's stomach tightened as an unnervingly explicit image popped into her mind. 'Trust you to think of sex!' Unfortunately, he wasn't the only one.

'I'm very trustworthy in that department.'

'I can imagine,' came her dry retort. 'But let's face it, Tyler, I'm a far cry from your usual choice of bedmate. For one thing, I don't measure up. I'm not nearly tall enough and I simply don't have the boobs.'

'Oh, I don't know…'

When his eyes dropped to her neat B-cup breasts, Michele was appalled to feel them tighten and tingle. Thank God she was wearing a lined jacket.

Despite this intensely irritating response, or perhaps because of it, Michele was suddenly consumed by curiosity over Tyler's abilities as a lover. He'd certainly had enough practice. But would his looks and wealth make him selfish and arrogant in bed? Or would he be as brilliant at sex as he was at everything else?

When Michele felt an embarrassing colour stealing into her face, her irritation metre zoomed right off the scale. Good Lord, what was the matter with her? Here she was, broken-hearted over Kevin, and thinking about sex with another man.

And not just any man, either. With *Tyler*, of all people!

'Oh, do stop this nonsense and come along,' she snapped, whirling to march back down the steps towards his car. 'I'm not in the mood to be teased by the likes of you, Tyler Garrison!'

'Pity. I was rather liking it.'

'Well, *stop*!' she ordered over her shoulder.

He gave her a mock salute. 'Yes, ma'am. Anything you say, ma'am.'

She stood at the passenger door and waited with toe-tapping impatience till he opened it for her, whereupon she did her best to lower herself gracefully into the low-slung seat. But it wasn't easy.

Michele always wore suits to work. Invariably black

and invariably with fitted jackets and short, rather tight skirts. Fitted jackets showed off her best feature, her tiny waist. And short, tight skirts, she'd found, made her legs look longer.

Short, tight skirts, however, weren't conducive to climbing into pavement-level passenger seats with any degree of ease or modesty. By the time she leant back and buckled up Michele was showing more leg than a swimsuit model.

Naturally Tyler noticed, if the direction of his gaze was anything to go by. But it wasn't Tyler leering at her legs which was bothering her so much, but her own sudden silly awareness of *him*.

She glared balefully his way. 'Not one word!'

His lips twitched a little. 'Wouldn't dream of it. Now, which way should I go?'

Out of the country, preferably, came the tart thought.

As Michele steeled herself to give Tyler directions she resolved not to have him stay for too long tonight. She was obviously in a weird and very vulnerable emotional state if she'd started thinking of him in such a deplorable fashion.

Shock, probably. And distress. It wasn't every day that you had to face the fact you'd been building your whole life around a false premise.

She'd been so sure, despite everything, that deep down Kevin loved her. As sure as she was that she loved him still.

Tears pricked her eyes once more.

Well, you were wrong, Michele, came the cruel voice of cold, hard reason. Dead wrong.

CHAPTER TWO

'THIS IS really nice, Michele,' Tyler said as he wandered around her L-shaped living/dining room.

Michele glanced at the simple and rather sparsely furnished apartment, with its polished wooden floors and matt cream walls, and couldn't for the life of her see any great reflection of her personality in the decor.

She hadn't had enough money left over from the hefty deposit she'd had to put down twelve months ago to indulge herself in the sort of expensive leather furniture she might one day buy. Instead, she'd spent several Saturdays going to auctions of deceased estates where she'd picked up a few bargains. She especially liked her mustard-yellow sofa and the two well-worn but deliciously comfortable brown leather recliners.

Tyler was settling himself in one of these at this very moment.

'And what does that mean?' she snapped, despite her vow down in the undercover car park to get a hold of this irrational irritation Tyler evoked in her once and for all.

But she'd always hated the word 'nice'. It was so very...nice.

Michele didn't feel nice at that moment. She felt angry and brittle and about to explode, or cry, or something!

'Nothing bad, I assure you,' he said as he crossed his ankles and leant back. 'I like the lack of clutter and fussiness. The bookcases are full of books, not tizzy ornaments. The pictures on the walls have something to say. They're not just there because they match the colours of the room. The furniture is simple and comfortable. Without pretence. Like you.'

It was a compliment, no doubt. So why couldn't she just accept it gracefully? Why did she have to hear a patronising tone in there somewhere? Why did she read 'without pretence' as meaning plain and rather boring?

Michele decided not to say a word; she just smiled a tight little smile and spun from where she'd been standing, watching him, ever since they'd come in.

That was another thing she always found herself doing whenever Tyler was around. Watching him. The way he looked and moved. The way he laughed and smiled. The way he dominated a room.

Still, in fairness to herself, it wasn't just *her* eyes which followed him around rooms. And it wasn't just women. Kevin had been drawn to him like a little puppy dog back during their university days, running after him wherever he went, looking up at him like an adoring cocker spaniel did its master.

Michele had hated that.

Kevin had become more his own man since then, but Michele still resented the power of Tyler's personality, and the unconsciously arrogant way he always expected people to do his bidding.

Marching into the kitchen, she dumped her shoulder

bag on the counter, only then remembering the totally mangled wedding invitation in her other hand. She ripped it open, then glared down at the contents, seeing that the wedding was to be at a church.

Outrage erupted within her. A church, for heaven's sake! Kevin had never graced a church in his life! At least, not since she'd known him. What a hypocrite! What a creep! What a…a…rotten, unfeeling, unfaithful bastard!

Tears welled up again as she shoved the hateful thing in the bin in the corner. Ten years of her life…wasted. Ten years of her life…consigned to the garbage.

She wanted to cry…quite desperately. But how could she, with Tyler sitting in the next room, smugly thinking that he'd warned her Kevin's character was flawed and would never give her what she wanted? She'd been waiting for Tyler to launch into the 'I told you so' ever since she'd invited him up here.

Dashing the tears away with the backs of her hands, she snatched up the electric kettle and shoved it under the tap. 'Instant coffee all right by you?' she called out through gritted teeth.

'Fine.'

'Turn on the television, if you'd like.'

'No, thanks. I'm content to just sit here and relax.'

Bully for you, she thought viciously. You just relax in there, Tyler, while I'm out here, valiantly hiding my broken heart and making you bloody coffee when what I really want to do is go in there and tell you to get the hell out of here so I can throw myself on my second-hand brass bed and cry my now opened eyes out.

But she didn't, of course. She went about getting two of her favourite earthenware mugs out of the cupboard, spooning in the instant coffee then adding a sweetener to hers while she dumped three heaped teaspoons of real sugar into Tyler's.

Tyler had a sweet tooth you wouldn't believe. His passion for desserts and chocolate and anything which had more than half a kilo of sugar in the recipe was phenomenal. Michele would never forget the day he'd eaten two whole toffee apples during a lecture recess, claiming the only way he could bear to eat fruit was to smother it in something sweet.

The most depressing part was that he never put on a pound, no matter how many cream cakes or chocolate cookies he stuffed down into his fantastically flat stomach. Kevin never ate cakes or biscuits, and he always had his coffee black and sugarless, because he had to watch his weight. Whenever he and Michele had lived together she'd gone to great lengths to cook him low-fat, low-calorie meals, because she knew how thingy he was about his body image.

Was it thinking about Kevin, or all the effort she'd put into pleasing him, which brought the tears back with a vengeance?

Michele didn't know. All she knew was that suddenly the dam wall she'd been trying so desperately to hold back had burst, and the flood was on.

She was standing there, clutching the kitchen sink and sobbing her heart out, when Tyler's large male hands curved over her shaking shoulders and drew her firmly back against the wall of his chest.

'It's all right,' he said gently. 'Cry all you want, if it makes you feel better. There's no one here but you and me…'

'Oh, Tyler!' she sobbed, and, whirling, wound her arms tight around his waist and hugged him for all she was worth.

It must have shocked him, for he froze for a moment or two before his own arms moved to wrap around her and hug her back, his head bending over hers, his lips brushing her hair. She quivered for a moment, then sobbed some more.

'There, there,' he crooned, within the warmth of the comforting cocoon he'd created for her. 'You'll get over this, Michele. I know you will.'

'But…but he's going to marry someone *else*!' she cried. 'I…I can't bear it. I love him so much.'

'Too much, Michele. You've always loved him too much.'

Resentment stirred within her distress. So he was back to that again, was he? Back to criticising her over Kevin. Why didn't he just give her a break?

Michele wrenched herself out of his arms and glared through soggy lashes up at him. 'What would *you* know about loving anyone too much?'

He glared back down at her, his beautiful blue eyes no longer sympathetic but hard and unforgiving. Tyler had never looked at her like that before, and it bothered her more than she liked to admit.

'I...I'm sorry,' she mumbled, sniffling a little. 'That was nasty of me.'

'Yes, Michele,' he agreed coldly. 'It was. Here. Wipe your nose on this.' Abruptly he handed her the gold silk pocket handkerchief which matched his tie.

She was happy to have the opportunity to look away from his chilling eyes. Even so, she could not let the subject drop, wanting perhaps to justify her remark. 'You...you have to admit you've never really been smitten with anyone,' she said while she wiped her nose. 'I mean...you have a different girlfriend every other week.'

When Tyler said nothing she dared to look up at him, and was relieved to see he was smiling again, that self-assured, faintly amused, wickedly sexy smile which was his trademark.

'You noticed, huh?'

'Hard not to.'

His shrug was nonchalant. 'Can't help it. I've never dated a girl who could hold my interest for very long.'

'Maybe that's because of the type of girl you choose to date,' she pointed out drily. 'I mean, let's face it, Tyler, they're not long on brains.'

'Maybe not.' He grinned. 'But they're long on legs.'

Michele began shaking her head at him. 'Tyler, Tyler, whatever am I going to do with you?'

'You could take pity on me and change my record.'

'Huh?'

'Come out to dinner and dancing with me tonight. That way I'll have dated a girl who has brains as well as great legs.'

Michele rolled her eyes at him. Nothing annoyed her more than when Tyler mocked her. Which was often. How could any girl have really great legs when she was only five foot two inches tall?

'Oh, sure. Dinner and dancing. With you. Right. Whatever you say, Tyler,' she mocked back.

Michele knew full well where a *real* date for dinner and dancing with Tyler was expected to end, and it wasn't being left at a girl's front door with a chaste kiss goodnight. She would be whisked back to the luxurious converted boat-house he lived in, down behind his parents' luxurious Vaucluse mansion, for a romp in his luxurious king-sized water bed.

'Good,' he said firmly. 'How long will it take you to get ready?'

She stared up at him for a second, then laughed, a little nervously. 'You're not serious.'

'Yes, I am. Quite serious.'

Michele was taken aback. For he even *sounded* serious.

The unexpected invitation brought a dart of undeniable and quite dizzying delight. Hadn't she always, down deep in some hidden compartment of her mind, dreamt about Tyler asking her out?

But he never had. Not once. He'd never even looked at her with a hint of desire, except a few minutes ago, down in the street and in his car.

But that hadn't been true lust. That had just been teasing on his part.

Yet here he was, asking her out on a date.

Any silly thrill swiftly faded once common sense

provided the real reason behind the invitation. This isn't going to be a *real* date, you ninny. Tyler simply feels sorry for you tonight because of Kevin. He's being...nice.

Michele winced at the word, and at a humiliating realisation. If she said yes, *she* would no doubt be delivered to her front doorstep at the end of the evening and given a chaste kiss goodnight.

Her already broken heart tightened with another, newer, sharper pain. The pain of feeling a total failure as a woman. Suddenly she felt not just unloved and un-needed, but totally unwanted. Even Kevin hadn't wanted her in the end, so why would Tyler? Brilliant, beautiful, breathtaking Tyler!

'Don't be silly,' she said, struggling not to sound irreversibly crushed. 'Ask someone else, if you're desperate for a night out. One of your bimbos with the inflatable boobs.'

'So you're saying no.'

The tight anger in his voice surprised her, till she realised how ungrateful she must have sounded.

'Look, it's very...sweet...of you to ask me out, Tyler, but I'm really too tired to go anywhere tonight. I had a hard day at work, and what with one thing and another, I just want to have a bite to eat here at home and go to bed fairly early.'

'Fair enough. What about another night, then?'

Michele sighed. 'Tyler, you really don't have to do this.'

'Do what?'

'You know what.'

'Ah, I see. You think I'm asking you out of pity.'

'Well, aren't you?'

His smile was rueful. 'I don't think I should answer that, lest I incriminate myself.'

Michele sighed, then turned back to the kitchen counter and the coffee. 'You still want this?' she threw over her shoulder at him.

'If it's not too much trouble...'

'How can making instant coffee be too much trouble? Go back and sit down in the lounge room. And put the TV on, would you? *Quick off the Mark* comes on at seven.'

'You like quiz shows?' Tyler asked when she came in with the two mugs and set them down on the coffee table.

'Yes, I do,' she said, and sat down in the other adjacent brown chair. *Usually*, she thought. But she didn't think she'd love anything much tonight.

'How about a competition?' Tyler suggested. 'Or aren't you game?'

His rather smug challenge sparked some spirit back into her and she slanted him an equally cocky look. 'Are you sure you'll be able to stand it when I beat the pants off you?'

If there was one thing she was good at, it was quiz shows. Her photographic memory had absorbed a massive amount of general knowledge and trivia over the years. She loved sitting there each evening, trying to answer the questions before the contestants did. Most of the time she succeeded.

He grinned. 'That depends on which pants you mean.'

Oh, truly! The man had a one-track mind. 'I'm speaking of hypothetical pants,' she said drily.

'Pity. Still, I think it will be *your* pants, madam, which had better be on guard.'

'Ooh…I'm terrified!'

'So you should be,' he said darkly, and Michele shot him a startled look. But he was smiling at her from behind his coffee mug and she realised he was just bantering with her. They bantered a lot, when they weren't arguing.

'Don't expect me to let you win,' he added, 'just because you're a woman.'

'Don't worry,' she returned drily. 'I don't. Now shush, the first question's coming up soon. We have to get our answer in before the contestant answers to count.'

'Natch.'

The next half-hour was the most fun Michele had had in simply donkey's ages! She won. But only just. Tyler was really good, especially on the longer 'Who am I?' questions. But she was quicker on the other parts, perhaps because she'd had more practice. Somehow Michele didn't think Tyler regularly stayed in to watch *Quick off the Mark* every night at seven o'clock, even if it was only on week nights.

When the show finally finished, and Tyler stood up to leave, she actually felt disappointed. A perverse situation, given she'd been dying for him to leave earlier.

Michele rose to her feet as well. 'If you'd like to

stay,' she suggested swiftly before he escaped, 'I could order a pizza. There's a special this month where you get two pizzas of your choice, some garlic bread, a Coke and an ice-cream cake for twenty dollars.'

'Mmm. Now that's an offer I simply *can't* refuse.'

Michele glared over at him. 'Are you being sarcastic? Look, I realise pizza is hardly your usual fare these days, but I can remember when you didn't mind slumming it with the rest of us. But I guess those good old days are well and truly over, aren't they?' she swept on, bending momentarily to snatch up the empty mugs. 'I suppose you don't open that silver-spoon mouth of yours nowadays except to put silver service food in it!'

'Oh, for Pete's sake!' Tyler exclaimed frustratedly. 'You know what you are, Michele? You're an inverted snob. And a right bitch sometimes. Now stop giving me a hard time and go order the damned pizza, or I'll put you over my knee and paddle that beautiful backside of yours, as all naughty girls should have them paddled.' And he sat back down in his chair.

Michele's face went bright red. She told herself it was anger at his last typical male remark. But she had an awful feeling it had something to do with the erotic image which had popped into her mind.

Good God, what on earth was wrong with her?

Whirling, she marched out to put the mugs in the kitchen, where she stayed for a while to regain her composure.

'I'm sorry,' she said briskly on her return. 'You're right. I don't know why you bother with me. Now that

I've split up with Kevin for good, I wouldn't blame you if you never rang me or took me to lunch ever again. I'm a difficult, ungrateful, impossible pain in the rear!'

'That's putting it mildly.'

'You don't have to rub it in,' she flared.

'Could I?'

He smiled. And she couldn't help it. She smiled back. It was very difficult to stay angry at Tyler when he decided to turn on the charm. Besides, it was herself she was most angry with.

'What say I get a video to go with those pizzas?' he suggested. 'One of those gloriously gung-ho good-guys-win-in-the-end movies we were all addicted to in the old days.'

'Okay.'

'Great!' He was on his feet in a flash. 'Now, who's your current favourite super-hero?'

'Whatever. You choose.'

'Wow! She can be agreeable when she wants to be.'

Michele's eyes narrowed. Her head cocked on one side, and her hands found her hips. 'I'll have you know I can be very agreeable when I want to be.'

'In that case you never seem to want to be with me.'

'Well, you do rub me up the wrong way some-times.'

'Why?'

'*Why?*'

'Yes. Why?'

'I...I don't really know,' she confessed, a little flustered by the question.

'Try to give me an answer, because I've always wanted to know. I won't be offended if you're brutally honest. After all,' he added wryly, 'you usually are.'

'Well...I guess it's because you're too...perfect.'

'Too *perfect*!' he exclaimed, then laughed. 'Honey, I'm far from perfect.'

'And I'm not really a bitch.'

Suddenly his face softened on her. 'I know,' he said. 'I'm sorry I said that too. You're a very warm, caring, loyal, genuine person. Kevin's a fool for letting you go.'

Michele agreed with him.

'But I think *you* were a *bigger* fool,' Tyler went on before she could preen too much, 'for putting up with him for so long.'

Michele opened her mouth to defend herself, but Tyler didn't give her the chance. 'I can understand why you fell for him in the first place. Kevin fooled all of us with his little-boy charm and self-deprecating modesty. I admit, I too liked the way he could make me feel with his endless flattery. Like I was someone very special. Someone he looked up to and relied upon. Someone who would always be there for him.'

Tyler hesitated, perhaps waiting for her to say something, but she was too startled and intrigued to say anything. Finally, he went on.

'He was king of the compliments, wasn't he? King of the sob-stories, too. But I finally worked out that both the sob-stories and the compliments were all designed to get Kevin what Kevin wanted, without any real effort of his own. When he grumbled about being dirt poor, then gushed over my car or my clothes, it was because he wanted to borrow them, or even for me to give them to him. When he told us all how much cleverer we were than he was, it was because he wanted us to do his assignments for him. Yes, I admit I fell for his wiles for some time myself. But not for ten years! I'd really love to know how he kept you blind for so long to the selfish, ambitious, money-grubbing little con-artist he really is, because whatever technique he used on you I'd like to bottle it! Or are you just a masochist by nature? Tell me! I'd love to know.'

Michele's mind reeled at such a vicious character assassination before her thoughts inexorably flew to the flattering things Kevin used to say to her all the time, even when they'd made love. He would shower her with compliments before and during and afterwards, making her try even harder to please him. She had ignored the fact that bells often didn't ring for her in bed, as long as they rang for him.

Dismay took hold as Michele realised that her love for Kevin had been as foolish and one-sided as Tyler had always said. So, yes…maybe she *was* a masochist. Because Kevin had delivered her more pain over the years than pleasure. In hindsight, she conceded, she'd become so addicted to the incredibly flattering things Kevin said she'd been prepared to ignore the dreadful things he did. What woman didn't want to hear that she was wonderful in bed; that she was the most beautiful, the most intelligent, the most understanding, the most warm and caring woman on the face of the earth?

When Kevin had first said such wonderful words she'd felt complete, as a female. He'd filled an empty space in her feminine soul which had been there as long as she could remember. When he'd repeated such seemingly sincere assertions during every attempted reconciliation she'd really wanted to believe him, because she'd wanted to feel that feeling again, that feeling of being valued and needed.

That was why she'd always taken him back, even when he'd caught the travel bug and left her for months at a time. Then when he'd caught a different kind of wanderlust. She'd let him have his affairs and still taken him back, because she'd told herself that that had only been sex. What they'd shared was deeper than sex. Much deeper.

But they hadn't shared a thing, she now accepted. She'd done all the giving and Kevin the taking. She'd done all the loving and the caring.

Tyler had called her a fool over Kevin, more than once. And he was right. Still, it was one thing to know something and quite another to face it, then move beyond it. Kevin had been a large part of her life for ten years, more than a third of her entire existence. It was going to be incredibly hard to forget him and move on.

But if she was to live with herself from this moment onwards, if she was to regain her self-esteem and have any pride at all…it had to be done!

'When's the wedding?' she asked abruptly.

Tyler looked startled. Had he been expecting her to rage back at him? There was some tension around his mouth, a mouth which might have looked feminine if it hadn't been balanced by a strong, straight nose and firmly squared jaw.

'Quite soon,' he said. 'The first Saturday in May. That's only three and a half weeks away. Why? Good God, Michele, surely you're not still hoping he'll break his engagement and come back to you!'

The thought had never occurred to her.

Even if he did, Michele knew she would never take Kevin back. Not again. Never, ever. For the first time since getting that wedding invitation she felt the beginnings of being in control.

It was a good feeling.

'Did your invitation say 'and partner'? she demanded of Tyler.

'Yes, I think so. Yes, I'm sure it did.'

'Do you have a steady girlfriend at the moment?'

'Er…not exactly a *steady* girlfriend.'

'Oh, I see. Just a playmate. In that case, the question is irrelevant. I'm sure whoever she is won't mind if you take an old friend to a wedding.'

Tyler's mouth came as close to dropping open as she'd ever seen it. 'You want me to take you to Kevin's wedding?'

'Would you?'

His expression was disbelieving. 'But why would you *want* to go?'

'Because I must.'

'I don't understand that decision, Michele,' he said ruefully. 'I really don't.'

Her smile was somewhat sad. 'My mother died of cancer when I was thirteen, Tyler. Did I ever tell you that?'

He frowned. 'No...no, I didn't know that. I mean...I knew she was dead, but not when or how. Still, what's that to do with going to Kevin's wedding?'

'When she died, I was asked if I wanted to view her body before the funeral, to say one last goodbye. I hadn't been allowed to visit her the last week. Dad had said she wouldn't know me because of the morphine. Anyway, in the end I didn't go and see her afterward, either. I told myself it was because I wanted to remember her when she was alive and well, but the truth was I was too afraid. Of what I might see. Of death. I've always regretted it. I... I...'

Her voice trailed off, and before she knew it Tyler was taking her into his arms again, and she was crying again.

'Oh, Michele...oh, honey...oh, please don't cry. And please don't think like that. You were only a young girl and she was your mum. I think you were wise not to go and see her like that. Much better to remember her as she was, like you said.'

'No, no, you don't understand,' Michele choked out, pulling away and lifting her tormented face to his. 'It would have made her death *real*. For years afterwards I never did quite believe it. I kept thinking she was just away somewhere. It was years before I came to terms with her being dead. Kevin marrying someone else is like a death for me. I need to be there, to watch him do it, to know that it's real, to see for myself what sort of man he really is. Then, afterwards, I'll be able to go on with my life without him.'

Tyler said nothing for a long time, just stroked the tears away from her cheeks with his fingertips.

At last, when she was fully composed again, he smiled down at her.

'In that case it would be my honour to take you,' he said gently. 'But with two provisos.'

'Anything.'

'Don't send an RSVP to your invitation.'

Michele's eyes widened at the thought of the shock Kevin would get on the day when he discovered her there, with Tyler.

'And the second proviso?' she asked, suddenly knowing why the desire for revenge was such a powerful emotion.

Tyler's eyes glittered. 'Wear something sexy…'

CHAPTER THREE

'WHAT DO YOU think?' Michele did a slow turn.

Lucille whistled. 'Wow. Aren't you glad you took me shopping with you? You look stunning in that colour. Even more so now, with your hair down and full make-up on.'

Michele stared at herself again in the dressing-table mirror and felt a real thrill of pleasure at her appearance.

When Lucille had first drawn the electric-blue outfit off the boutique rack last Saturday, she'd shaken her head and said it was too bright. She never wore bright colours, mostly opting for neutrals. Neutrals were far more user-friendly when it came to mixing and matching, *and* for wearing an outfit many times. Being of a practical nature, Michele always bypassed bright colours when it came to clothes.

But Lucille had shoved it in her hands and insisted she try it on. The rest was history. Now, here she was, dressed from head to toe in electric blue, nerves gathering in the pit of her stomach as she wondered what Kevin would say when he saw her.

Before Kevin, however, would come Tyler. Odd, she thought, but she was actually more nervous over what Tyler would think of her appearance than Kevin.

'Something sexy', he'd asked for. What she was

40

wearing was certainly that, as well as being soft and elegant and far more feminine than anything she'd ever worn before.

A layered outfit, it had a figure-hugging ankle-length satin sheath underneath and a long-sleeved chiffon coat-dress on top, secured across her bodice by a series of tiny jet buttons. When she walked, the chiffon fell apart from her waist and floated out behind her whilst the slender satin underskirt hugged her stomach and thighs.

'I won't get my money's worth out if it,' she said, though not really caring. It was worth the exorbitant price tag to look like this.

'Your playboy friend is in for a shock when he sees you,' Lucille commented drily. 'I do hope you know what you're doing, asking someone like him to take you to Kevin's wedding. No matter how much in control you say you are, you're bound to get all teary afterwards. He'll put his big bad wolf arms around you, and before you know it, you'll be in bed with him.'

Michele had to laugh. 'If you knew Tyler, you'd know how ridiculous that is. He doesn't fancy me that way. Not one iota. We're just good friends.'

'And that's the most overworked and underestimated phrase in the English language! How could any red-blooded man not fancy you, looking the way you look today? Believe me, sweetie, you're going to be hit on by every single guy at the reception, not to mention all the creepy married ones. Even if our esteemed Mr Garrison hasn't looked at you that way before today, he's about to make a major reassessment.'

'I'll believe *that* when I see it.'

'Oh, you won't see it. It'll creep up on you, just like he will, being a big bad wolf.'

'You don't know Tyler. For your information, I've already been teary with him about Kevin. *And* been taken into his big bad wolf arms. Twice!'

'Oooh. Do tell. What happened?'

'Nothing. He gave me his hanky to blow my nose on, said a few comforting words, then left.'

'Oh…' Lucille looked almost disappointed for a moment. 'Oh, well, that's good, then. As I said, you can never be too careful where men are concerned. Especially when it comes to sex.'

'Tyler has more sex than he can handle. He certainly doesn't need to seduce little ole me.'

'So, when is Tyler due to pick you up? You said the wedding's scheduled for four o'clock? And it's at some trendy old church in North Chatswood?'

'I told him I'd be waiting downstairs in the foyer for him at three-thirty.'

Tyler had called her every so often to see how she was, and if she still wanted to go to the wedding—the last time three nights ago. By then she'd bought the dress and nothing would have stopped her, short of death or war. She hadn't heard from Kevin. Not a word, even when she hadn't replied to *her* invitation.

Michele still could not believe Kevin could treat her so shabbily. Why send her an invitation at all, if he wanted nothing more to do with her? She could only think he was being deliberately cruel.

Lucille glanced at her watch. 'It's three-fifteen now. Let's do a checklist. Got your perfume on?'

'Yes.'

'Jewellery?'

'No. No jewellery.' Her hair covered her ears and she hadn't been able to find a necklace which suited.

'You're right,' Lucille agreed. 'That dress doesn't need adornment. Shoes?'

Michele gave her a droll look. 'Hard to miss them, don't you think?' The current fashion leant towards scandalously high and very strappy shoes for evening wear, and Michele had given in to buying a black patent pair of vertigo-inspiring dimensions...at Lucille's instigation again. They were a far cry from the sensible black pumps Michele usually wore, so she'd been practising in them every evening this past week. No way did she want to totter around like a drunken idiot at Kevin's wedding. Or fall over some pew or other.

'Great shoes!' Lucille praised for the umpteenth time. 'Pity your feet are smaller than mine. Otherwise I'd be borrowing them all the time. Purse all packed?' she went on. 'Got your money, keys, perfume, lippy, tissues, condoms?'

Michele rolled her eyes at her friend, who didn't look at all embarrassed.

Lucille shrugged. 'Okay, so I'm not an optimist when it comes to the opposite sex. So shoot me.'

Michele dropped the aforementioned essentials— minus the condoms—into her black patent evening purse. She didn't own any condoms, anyway. Maybe there was an isolated one in a bathroom drawer somewhere. She recalled seeing it one day whilst tidying up.

Kevin had always attended to protection. He'd been fanatical about it.

Naturally. He'd probably been cheating on her right from the start. Con-men had to be clever, *and* careful. Or they got caught.

'I agree with you where men are concerned,' she said sourly as she shot the zipper along the top of the clutch purse. 'But you're talking about me here, too, Lucille. And I've never been into casual sex.'

'There's a first time for everything. And the day the bloke you're madly in love with marries someone else just might be the day, don't you think?'

Michele's hand tightened around her black evening purse and Lucille gave her a stricken look. 'Oh, God, I'm sorry, Michele. What a stupid thing for me to say when you're being so brave. I'd like to shoot *myself* now!'

'No, it's all right,' Michele reassured her, conceding that the comment hadn't caused as much distress as it would have a month ago. In the weeks since she'd received the wedding invitation she'd done a lot of thinking. And she'd come to the conclusion that Kevin had become an unhealthy habit, one which she'd found impossible to break till he'd done it for her.

Love had an insidious way of making one blind to the truth. And to one's own flaws. She'd been weak to take Kevin back so many times. Weak and wishy-washy.

Yet she wasn't a weak or wishy-washy person in any other department of her life. She'd never put her head in the sand about anything or anyone, except Kevin.

She wondered what he thought she might be doing today…if he thought of her at all, that was! Did he imagine her crying in a corner somewhere? If he did, then he was about to get the shock of his life! Because she wouldn't be in any corner. She would be right there, letting him see she would survive without him; that he wasn't the axis of her world any more; that she would never take him back, no matter what.

Michele knew that showing up with Tyler would go a long way to achieving that end. If Kevin thought she was actually *dating* Tyler, then so much the better. He wouldn't like that at all.

Mmm. Perhaps she could ask Tyler to let him think they were…

'Michele?' Lucille prompted. 'Say something. Don't just stand there, looking odd.'

Michele flashed her friend a reassuring smile. 'I'm fine,' she said.

Lucille didn't look convinced. 'You're sure?'

'Yes. My eyes are well and truly opened now. Kevin didn't deserve me, the creep. I'm well rid of him.'

'I could have told you that, if you'd asked me.'

'Tell me now.'

'He didn't deserve you, the creep, and you're well rid of him!'

Michele smiled. 'Thanks. Now I'd better get going. For a playboy, Tyler's notoriously punctual.'

Lucille walked with her down to the foyer, where they waited and watched through the glass front doors for Tyler's car to appear at the kerb. It was a little breezy to wait outside, Michele not wanting her expensive hairdo to blow to bits. She'd had it done that morning at a salon down in Greenwood Plaza, where they'd brilliantly transformed her straight, shoulder-length brown bob into a slinky style which would not have gone astray in a film *noir* from the forties. Parted on one side, and with the fringe brushed back off her forehead, her hair now curved around her face and neck in sexy bangs and waves, before resting on her shoulders in a glossy curtain. It was a sexy look, to go with the sexy dress.

Three-thirty came and went, with no sign of Tyler.

At three-forty Michele was considering going back upstairs and ringing Tyler's mobile when a shiny green sedan screeched to a halt outside, the man himself leaping out from behind the wheel.

'Don't tell me he's bought another new car!' Michele exclaimed in exasperation.

'Who cares about the car?' Lucille retorted. 'Just look at that gorgeous hunk of male flesh! Did you ever see anything so beautiful in all your life?'

Michele could well understand Lucille's lascivious admiration. Tyler in a tux was a sight to behold.

In a way, Lucille's reaction was a comfort. It explained why Michele's own heart was racing a little. Tyler was one of those men who automatically tripped a woman's sexual starter gun.

'If I was into blond men, I'd wangle an invitation,' Lucille muttered as Tyler strode towards the front steps. 'But, to be honest, I like my men dark and brooding. Still, I wish you'd taken notice of me and let me slip a couple of condoms into your purse. I mean…golly, girl, if you're not quite over Kevin yet, then that's just the sort of medicine to complete the cure.'

'What?' Michele gaped at her friend.

'Come on, Michele, he'd give you a tumble if you asked him.'

'Lucille! Up in my apartment you were warning me off Tyler! Now you're telling me to proposition him! Have you gone stark raving mad?'

'On second thoughts, you're quite right. That was a crazy suggestion. You're not the sort of girl who could handle something like that. Forget I said it. Now I'm outta here. Don't want to steal any of your thunder. Bye!'

Lucille made a dash for the stairs, leaving Michele to try to forget Lucille's outrageous suggestion and re-gather a degree of composure. But as she hurried through the glass security doors all she could do was stare at Tyler walking towards her and wonder what he would say if she *did* ask him to take her to bed tonight.

Her gaze swept down his elegantly clad body, then back up to his face, that classically handsome face with its superb bone structure, piercing blue eyes and sexy, full-lipped mouth. The thought of that mouth on hers, then on other more intimate parts of her body sent her heartbeat skittering wildly, her fluster not helped when *he* ground to a halt and gave *her* a startled once-over.

'My God! Michele!' Taking both her hands, he held them out wide, his eyes sweeping down her satin-clad body once more, then up again, landing on what she hoped was an unflushed face. 'What can I say?' he pronounced, smiling broadly. 'You look good enough to eat!'

It was the wrong thing to say in view of what she'd recently been thinking. Instantly her mind flew to imagine his doing just that, an activity which she'd always wondered about, yet never actually experienced. Not for longer than three seconds, anyway.

'That colour on you is just so…scrumptious,' he added.

'Thank you,' she managed to reply, though her voice sounded raw and husky.

'We'd better hurry or we'll miss the big event. Sorry I was late. Had to pick up my new car. Er…watch these steps in those stilts you're wearing. Don't want you falling on your face before the groom-to-be sees his revamped ex.'

Tyler's drily amused words sent her mind whipping back from fantasy land to cold, hard reality. No matter how…scrumptious…she might look, Tyler's feelings for her were not about to be reassessed. He'd never fancied her and he wasn't about to start!

'They happen to be the latest in fashion,' she told him tartly.

'Maybe. But they're a decided dancing hazard. You'll need an expert partner to keep you off other toes tonight. Which means no dancing with anyone else but yours truly tonight. Oh, that reminds me. I thought we might let Kevin think we'd become an item since last we met. Give him a taste of his own medicine.'

A flabbergasted Michele sent him a surprised look. 'Do you know, I was going to ask you to pretend we were really dating?'

Tyler looked surprised as well. 'Were you now? Well, great minds think alike, you know.'

'Then you wouldn't mind?'

'Mind? Why should I mind?'

Michele supposed she wouldn't be an embarrassment to him looking as she did today. 'What about your girlfriend?'

'What girlfriend?'

'The one you... Oh, I see...' Michele sighed. 'That was more than three weeks ago. An eternity in your dating life. So she's gone the way they've all gone, has she? The same as the Jag.'

Tyler shrugged, then bent to open the car door for her. 'I gave her a going away present,' he elaborated as he helped her into the far more user-friendly passenger seat. 'Believe me, she wasn't broken-hearted.'

'Tyler, you're a wickedly shallow man when it comes to women.'

'Till now,' he agreed. 'But change is in the wind.'

'I'll believe that when I see it,' she scoffed, snapping her seat belt into place.

'I hope so,' he said, straightening to stand by her still opened door.

'I won't hold my breath!'

When he made no further retort, Michele glanced up, taken aback to find Tyler staring down at her with a faintly troubled expression. But then he smiled down at her in that sardonic fashion which was so irritatingly familiar, slammed the car door and strode round to the driver's side.

'I see I'll have to re-educate you where I'm concerned,' he told her in mock seriousness once he'd climbed in and belted himself up. 'Show you what a wonderfully warm, deeply sincere, incredibly sensitive man I really am.'

Michele tried not to laugh, but it bubbled up out of her. 'Oh, Tyler! Truly, you're a classic!'

She was still laughing when Tyler turned the ignition key and drove off in a pretend huff.

CHAPTER FOUR

MICHELE'S laughter had long died by the time they arrived at the church, nerves re-gathering in the pit of her stomach. As luck would have it, the bride was running late, but everyone else had filed inside, leaving them to enter to the twisting stares of all the other guests.

Michele's arm tightened around Tyler's for the walk down the aisle in search of a spare pew.

All the women stared at Tyler as they passed by, which was only to be expected. Michele, however, had to endure some skin-crawling stares of her own from several trendily dressed yuppie males, none of whom she recognised, not even on Kevin's side.

Probably new business and social contacts, met through the bride. Kevin didn't have any close relatives to invite. Or if he did he'd never made mention of them.

Michele was grateful his mother had passed away a couple of years back, because she surely wouldn't have been invited, either, that poor, maligned creature who'd given birth to Kevin out of wedlock and never been allowed to forget it by her illegitimate son. She'd committed the huge crime of bringing up Kevin on an unmarried mother's allowance, living in a housing commission flat out in the outer western suburbs.

Michele had once felt sorry for Kevin when he'd complained about his childhood. Now she wondered if he was just an ungrateful wretch!

Kevin himself, thank heavens, was not yet standing at the head of the aisle. Now that Michele was actually here, she wished she wasn't. But it was too late now.

The organ started up and the minister emerged from the sacristy, followed by Kevin and two other men, all dressed in black dinner suits. Michele stared at the man she'd loved all these years and tried to see him objectively for once, without being swayed—or fooled—by old wants and old needs.

He looked sharp, she had to admit. And quite handsome. But it was a handsomeness which would fade, his soft face and fleshy frame lacking the superb bone structure which lasted into middle age and beyond.

Still, Michele had once been drawn to Kevin's boyish good looks, not to mention his seeming softness.

Even now, as she looked him over with what she hoped was a more pragmatic view, her inner self flooded with conflicting feelings. Her mind condemned him whole-heartedly, but her stupid female heart still contracted at the thought he was turning his back on true love for the sake of money. He didn't love Danni. She was sure of it.

Oh, Kevin…

Perhaps sensing her gaze on him, he looked her way and their eyes met. His widened a little, then widened some more when he saw whose arm she was clutching.

Michele felt no satisfaction in witnessing his shocked reaction at seeing her there with Tyler. No sense of triumph. Nothing but an overwhelming flood of misery. People always said revenge was bittersweet. Well, in this case it was more bitter than sweet.

The organ bursting forth with the 'Bridal March' sent Kevin's momentarily stunned gaze wrenching back to the aisle, where his beautiful blonde bride was floating towards him on a dream of lace and tulle. Immediately he smiled at her, one of those warmly intimate just-for-you smiles which had once made Michele's heart melt on cue.

Her fingers dug into Tyler's arm at the sight of the bride's answering smile, and the realisation he would never smile at her that way again. How could she bear it, hearing Kevin promise to love and cherish another woman; witnessing their union being blessed; watching him kiss her afterwards?

'We can leave if you want to?' Tyler whispered.

Michele was tempted. But leaving equated with running away in her mind. And she'd been a coward where Kevin was concerned long enough.

'No,' she bit out. 'I'm staying.'

And stay she did.

Strangely, as the minutes passed things improved, perhaps because she willed herself into a frozen state, devoid of all emotion or movement. She didn't even flinch when Kevin kissed his bride. By the time the register-signing part was over and people began filing from their pews to follow the happy couple outside, Michele was totally numb.

'Time to go,' Tyler murmured, giving her a small nudge in the ribs.

'Oh…' The smiling face mask she'd been wearing cracked as she stood up, and her legs momentarily went to jelly. Tyler's firm hand on her elbow provided much needed support, and she raised only slightly moist eyes to him.

'Thank you,' she choked out. 'I'll never forget this, or how kind you've been. You're a true friend, Tyler.'

He said nothing for once, just smiled a small smile and patted her arm.

A watery sun greeted them outside, where Michele was grateful that the wedding group was fully occupied having photographs taken in the nicely kept grounds.

'What about the reception?' Tyler asked as he steered her carefully down the old stone steps. 'Are you still determined to go to that as well?'

'Yes, I am,' came her steely reply.

'Good. I want to see the bastard squirm some more.'

Michele stopped at the foot of the steps, her eyes jerking up to stare at him. 'You sound like you hate Kevin.'

'I do,' he pronounced, and his eyes were colder and harder than she'd ever seen them.

'But why? What's he ever really done to you?'

'He's a user,' he pronounced. 'I don't like users.'

'Hello, Tyler.'

The woman's voice came from behind Michele's shoulder and she had to turn to see its owner, her heart sinking when she saw it belonged to Tyler's sister, Cleo, looking like a million dollars in a silvery grey dress and jacket.

A female version of Tyler with his fair good looks, Cleo was his only sibling, a few years younger than her brother and still single. Michele had met her several times at Tyler's parties and had always gained the impression Cleo didn't like her. Why, she wasn't sure.

'Hi, there, sis,' Tyler replied. 'I'm surprised to see you here. Didn't realise you knew old Kev that well.'

'I'm on the bride's side,' she returned, in that cut-glass voice of hers.

Michele had always liked it that Tyler talked like an Australian, and not with the pseudo-plummy accent common amongst Sydney's society set.

'Danni and I went to school together,' Cleo elaborated, before turning her ice-blue eyes Michele's way. 'Hello, there, Michele. Now *you're* the one I'm really surprised to see here. You brought her, Tyler?'

Michele bristled at the unspoken disapproval in Cleo's tone. So did Tyler, if the stiffening in his hand on her elbow was anything to go by.

'Any reason I shouldn't?' came his clipped retort.

'I doubt Danni will be happy with Kevin's ex being at their wedding.'

'Don't be ridiculous,' Tyler snapped. 'Michele was invited—she broke up with Kevin months ago.'

Cleo's face was still displaying disapproval when the groom himself joined the trio, inserting himself forcefully between Michele and Tyler, then linking arms with them both, a wide smile on his face.

'Well, if it isn't my two best buddies from uni, here together to see me tie the knot!' Kevin said, in the boldest display of sheer gall Michele had ever witnessed. 'And there I was thinking you'd forgotten me, Michele. Naughty girl, not sending an RSVP. I didn't realise you were coming with Tyler. But I'll forgive you since you're looking so gorgeous today. As for you, Tyler…I'm not sure I'll forgive *you* for not coming to my stag party the other night. You really missed something, buddy. I hope what you were doing instead was worth it. Or should I say I hope *she* was worth it?' And he laughed in a nudge-nudge, wink-wink, say-no-more fashion.

This was all news to Michele. Tyler had never said anything about Kevin asking him to his stag party.

'I certainly think so,' Tyler replied suavely. 'I was taking Michele out to dinner and dancing.' And he smiled at her, a warm, sexy, dazzling smile which knocked her for six…till she'd remembered that they'd agreed to pretend to be genuinely dating.

The *blasé* expression on Kevin's face faded, whilst Tyler's sister simply glared at her, then at her brother.

'Are you saying that you and Michele are actually going out together?' Cleo demanded to know.

'Yes. Why?' Tyler countered coolly. 'You got a problem with that?'

Michele could see Cleo battling not to say anything she shouldn't in front of others. 'No,' she said stiffly. 'No, of course not. It was just a surprise, that's all. You hadn't mentioned it before.'

'It's a relatively new development. Isn't it, Michele?'

'Er…yes,' she agreed, trying not look guilty. But she'd never been a good actress. Tyler, however, was very convincing. He'd starred in the videos their group had made back at university, and been excellent. With his looks and talent he probably could have made a career in the movies.

'For which I have *you* to thank, Kevin,' he went on blithely. 'If you hadn't broken up with Michele she'd never had gone out with me and I'd never have known what a truly remarkable woman she was. All these years I thought I knew her, but I didn't. Not really. Being a friend is simply not the same as being a girl-friend. And I think she'd say the same about me. Now that you really know me, darling—and I'm not just talking about in the biblical sense—I don't irritate you like I used to, do I?'

Michele did her best not to give away the game. But Tyler really *was* a wicked man when he wanted to be. Calling her darling like that and insinuating that they'd been intimate. The very idea! Still, she found she rather liked the look on Kevin's face, the mixture of shock and jealousy. Maybe revenge could be sweet after all!

'Only sometimes,' she murmured.

'There! See? I used to irritate her *all* the time. Ah, Kev, mate, I think your bride is looking for you. Off you go, buddy. You have to toe the line now that you're an old married man. No more orgies or all night drinking sessions for you!'

Once a sour-faced Kevin had been dragged off by his bride, there remained only Cleo to deal with. Tyler smiled at his sister whilst snaking an arm around Michele and drawing her close to his side.

'See, sis? Everything's cool. No problems at all.'

She smiled a rueful smile in return. 'It's early days yet, brother dear. Very early days. I dare say I'll be seeing more of you, Michele. Bye for now.'

And she walked off.

Her parting shot bothered Michele. 'What did she mean by that?' she asked Tyler.

'Nothing. She's being a typical sister. Thinks she knows it all. But she doesn't.'

'Neither do I, obviously. I'm very confused.'

'Cleo believes what we said, that we're genuinely dating. She's merely assuming I'll be bringing you home for dinner and dos and things.'

'What are you going to tell her when you don't?'

'I'll cross that bridge when I come to it.'

'And that's your whole philosophy on life, isn't it? You take each day as it comes. You don't worry about anything.'

'I wouldn't say that, exactly. But worry won't change things. Constructive action might. Now! Are you feeling better than when you were in the church?'

'Actually…yes,' she said, surprised to find that her depression had definitely lifted.

'So you're ready to face the reception?'

'I will be after I've downed a few cocktails.'

'Getting drunk won't solve anything.'

'Maybe not, but it makes things look better.'

'I hope I won't have to carry you up the stairs tonight.'

'You agreed to bring me here today,' she reminded

him. 'And it was *your* idea we pretend it was a real date. You'll just have to suffer the consequences.'

'And the consequences could be a plastered Michele whom I'll have to undress and put to beddy-byes at the end of the night?' His blue eyes sparkled with wicked amusement as they raked down her electric-blue dress, then up again. 'Mmm. What a simply terrible thought!'

Michele knew he was just teasing her, but colour still stole into her cheeks. Lucille really had a lot to answer for, putting such scandalous ideas into her head!

'Stop that nonsense and let's get out of here,' she said swiftly, before he noticed her blushing.

'Yes, ma'am. Straight to the reception, ma'am? Which way should I go, ma'am?'

Michele pursed her lips and eyed him with total exasperation. 'Anyone would think I was a bossy-boots, the way you carry on sometimes.'

'You *are* a bossy-boots. And a control freak. Not to mention madly ambitious and competitive.'

'Oh, really!' she said, crossing her arms and giving him a killer look. 'Do go on, Dr Freud. Do I have *any* redeeming qualities?'

'Absolutely not,' he replied, with a perfect poker face. 'Not by modern standards. People these days don't value virtues like honesty and loyalty. They despise people who work hard and want to get on in the world. They have no time for punctuality or professionalism. They prefer shallow, weak, superficial, lazy, lying, cheating, drug-taking slobs. So, no,

Michele...I'm afraid you don't have any redeeming qualities at all.'

Michele shook her head at him. 'I'm not sure how to take that. Are you mocking me or complimenting me?'

He smiled a wry, cryptic little smile. 'I'm telling you the truth...if you want to hear it.'

'And what does *that* mean?'

'It means it's time for me, as your date for the evening, to drive you to the reception, get you plastered, then take you home to bed.'

Michele's heart jumped into her mouth. Till the devilish gleam in his eyes gave him away.

Tyler was teasing her.

Again.

Well, two could play at that game!

'Good idea,' she purred instead. 'Hop to it, then, Tyler darling. And don't spare the horses!'

CHAPTER FIVE

THE RECEPTION was being held in a magnificent old mansion at Mosman, refurbished a decade earlier to be used for grand functions which naturally included society weddings. A two-storeyed stone structure with wide balconies and elegant lacework railings, it had an acre of rolling lawns out at the front, and parking for a hundred cars at the back.

Tyler swung his new car—a Honda Legend—into a space between a navy Mercedes and a zippy silver number, the tyres crunching on the gravel surface.

'I don't know whether to take my purse with me or not,' Michele said once it was time to get out. 'What do you think, Tyler?'

'Leave it. If you need a comb, I'll lend you mine.'

'Good thinking.'

By the look of the car park, most of the guests had already arrived—a distinct possibility since Tyler had driven here from the church far slower than usual. Michele had a feeling he no more wanted to be at this reception than she did. There was an air of reluctant resignation about him as he linked his arm with hers and headed towards the front of the house.

To all intents and purposes, however, they both walked quite boldly up the wide stone steps and through the opened double doors, where a uniformed

61

flunky directed them towards a sweeping staircase which reminded Michele of the one in the film *Gone With The Wind*. On their way towards it she noted a narrow table along the wall to her left which was piled high with elaborately packaged wedding presents. Despite everything, her omission to buy the happy couple a small gift—or even a card—struck deep at her conscience.

'It's all right,' Tyler murmured, steering her past the table and up onto the first red-carpeted step. 'I had my secretary buy them something suitably expensive. It was delivered to the bride's home yesterday. So there's no need to feel guilty.'

She stopped to throw him a startled look. 'How did you know what I was thinking?'

'I always know what you're thinking,' he said drily. 'Your eyes have this depressing habit of being unable to hide the truth. How do you think I knew I irritated the death out of you most of the time? Frankly though, Michele, if you're to continue your career in advertising you'll have to develop the ability to dissemble a little more.'

'You mean I have to learn to lie?'

'Not lie, exactly. But a little harmless pretence wouldn't go astray. Life can be cruel to those who are too honest and who wear their hearts on their sleeves.'

'You mean like I have with Kevin...'

'Exactly. Since you've come here today to have done with the man once and for all, best he really believes that's the case, Michele, or he might be back on your doorstep one day, married or not.'

'He'd better not!'

'And if he does come crawling back, telling you his wife doesn't understand him, that it's you he really loves and you he still wants, what will you do?'

'I... I... I...'

'I love a girl who knows her own mind.'

His wearily cynical tone sparked an indignant fury within her. 'It's all very well for you to be judge and jury when you don't care about anyone. You can't possibly know what it feels like to love someone as long as I've loved Kevin!'

'I think I can imagine...'

'No, you couldn't. You simply have no idea. But to answer your question, now that I've had time to think about it, I would not have anything more to do with him. Kevin belongs to another woman now and I...I belong to no one but myself!' She drew herself up straight, her chin tilting up. 'I know I've been a fool over him. You don't have to tell me any more. But I will not be a fool over him again. I can promise you that.'

He stared down into her proudly determined eyes for what felt like ages, as though waiting for her to break. But she didn't, and finally he bent to give her the sweetest, softest kiss.

Her lips quivered underneath his, her heart jolting.

'And what was that for?' she demanded to know.

He shrugged. 'Just for being you.'

She was touched, but at the same time confused. Because all of a sudden she wanted him to kiss her again, not so sweetly or softly this time. She wanted to feel his lips taking hers with passion, not compassion. She wanted his mouth crashing down on hers and obliterating all her pain, showing her that she wasn't a failure as a woman, that she was beautiful and sexy and he wanted her, even if only momentarily.

Dear heaven, she must be going crazy!

When Tyler suddenly snaked a hand around her waist and pulled her hard against him, Michele was so taken aback that she just stood there, stunned, staring up at him. Had he read her mind? she wondered dazedly. Surely he wasn't really going to kiss her...

When his other hand slid under the curtain of her hair and cupped the nape of her neck, every fibre of her being tightened. He *was* going to kiss her!

'Kevin and his bride have just come in the front door,' he whispered as his mouth slowly began to descend. 'I can't think of anything better to persuade Kevin that you've moved on from him than to see you kissing me. *Really* kissing me, honey.'

Michele was momentarily torn between anger and dismay. She should have known it was just part of the pretence. But then his lips met hers and every wretched self-pitying thought in her head scattered, leaving her with nothing to concentrate on but Tyler's mouth on hers, kissing her as though he were a man just emerged from a year in a desert and she was the coolest, sweetest spring. He sipped for a second or two, then sought to drink his fill, urging her trembling lips apart and sending his tongue deep into the well of her mouth.

Michele would have gasped if she could. But it was

impossible with Tyler's tongue filling her mouth. Instead, an abandoned-sounding moan escaped her throat.

She tried telling herself that Tyler's seeming passion was only pretence, but then his fingers moved with tantalising sensuality against the soft skin of her neck and she began kissing him back with a fervour which was positively indecent, considering she was still in love with another man. When Tyler's hand in the small of her back pressed her even closer, she didn't resist in the slightest, revelling in the feel of his hard male body moulding to hers. She didn't even care that the buttons on his jacket were digging painfully into her breasts, or that his belt buckle was...

Shock rippled down Michele's spine as she realised it wasn't Tyler's belt buckle pressing into her stomach. Not unless it was a very big, long sword-shaped buckle.

Abruptly he wrenched his mouth away, their lips breaking apart with a startled sucking noise.

'See, darling?' Danni purred from somewhere near. 'No need to worry about Michele any longer. She seems to have recovered from her broken heart by the look of things.'

A dazed Michele looked over at Kevin, who was staring back at her with disbelieving eyes.

'You could be right, Danni,' Tyler returned smoothly. 'Either that or she's the best actress since Bette Davis.'

'Michele can't act to save her life,' Kevin bit out.

'Really?' Tyler drawled. 'That's a comfort to know.'

'Come along, Danni,' Kevin said stiffly, taking his bride's arm. 'The photographer wants us upstairs for some shots on the front balcony. I'll see you two love-birds later,' he said, throwing both of them forced smiles.

'And is he right?' Tyler asked as soon as they'd gone.

Michele could hardly look at him for thinking about the way she'd kissed him, and the way he'd responded. 'What...what about?'

'Your acting ability.'

What was it he wanted her to say? A flustered confusion wormed its way into her stomach when he continued to stare down at her with eyes which told her of his own puzzlement.

But was it her kissing him like that which puzzled him the most? Or his own unlikely arousal?

Dismay claimed her at the thought it was probably the latter. Dismay and resentment.

'You told me to really kiss you,' she threw at him. 'You said I had to learn to dissemble. So I did! So stop asking stupid questions. I can't help it if you're a sex maniac who gets turned on at the drop of a hat.'

'I wouldn't describe what you did as the drop of a hat,' he said drily. 'You're some kisser, Michele. If that's just a taste of your abilities in the bedroom, then I'm beginning to see why dear old Kev kept coming back.'

'If I'm so darned good in bed then why did he leave me in the first place?'

'You haven't worked that out yet?'

'No, Mr Smarty-Pants, I haven't!'

'Aside from the money angle, he simply couldn't compete.'

'Compete with whom?'

'With you, darling heart. Now, let's go upstairs and get on with killing off this one-sided relationship once and for all. I've finally grown bored with it.'

'You and me both,' she muttered, shrugging off his hand when he tried to take her arm again. 'Why on earth do you have to keep touching me? I'm quite capable of negotiating stairs under my own steam, thank you very much. I'm not an invalid, just an idiot!'

'You said it. I didn't.'

'You don't have to. You've been telling me for years. So take a bow, Tyler. I'm finally admitting you're right. Feel better now?'

'Much,' he said, and smiled down at her.

She didn't want to smile back. But she did, wryly. Truly, the man was a menace, with far too much charm and sex appeal for his own good. No wonder women threw themselves at him. Lord, she herself had succumbed with amazing swiftness, seduced by a pretend kiss.

Though there'd been nothing pretend about what she'd felt pressing into her stomach...

Not that that meant anything, she reminded herself irritably. Men were renowned through history for being turned on by anything from the glimpse of an ankle to still-life pictures of fruit! How much more easily could their carnal appetites be revved up by a real live French kiss? It didn't mean Tyler fancied her any more than he ever had.

As for herself...well, she was just vulnerable tonight, as Lucille had pointed out, suffering from a bad case of terminal rejection. She'd been temporarily overcome by need there for a moment—the need to feel desirable and wanted. There was no need to make a big deal out of it. Tyler certainly wouldn't be.

'Maybe I *do* need some assistance after all,' she said with a return to common sense, lifting the hem of her dress with her right hand whilst sliding her left through the crook of Tyler's nearest arm. 'Getting up these stairs in this long tight skirt and these shoes might present some difficulty.'

'So glad to be of help, ma'am.'

'Oh, do stop being unctuous. It doesn't suit you.'

When he laughed, she finally laughed with him.

The staircase led up to a large landing off which a wide hallway ran straight ahead, opening out onto the front balcony. The sounds of voices and glasses clinking directed them down this hallway, past twin powder rooms and to a large room on the left which was chock-full of people standing around in groups and being served pre-dinner drinks and hors d'oeuvres.

Michele didn't think she'd ever seen so many expensively dressed yuppies in one place at the one time.

'Stick by my side,' Tyler advised as they entered and all male eyes immediately flicked her way. 'Unless, of course, you want to spend all evening warding off the flies. And I don't mean the buzzing kind.'

Though Michele chuckled, she soon saw what he meant. Over the next hour an amazing number of suave pseudo-seducers insinuated themselves into their company, all of them wanting to chat her up and using every trick in the book to angle her away from Tyler and into a private corner for Lord knows what.

But they were subtle compared to what the females did in pursuit of Tyler. They were absolutely shame-less in their more-than-flirtatious intentions, giving Michele a glimpse of what he had to put up with most of the time.

She clung to his arm tighter and tighter, afraid to leave his side even to go to the powder room, though after several champagne cocktails she really needed to. In the end she excused herself and made a bolt for the Ladies', resigned to the fact that the moment she left Tyler alone great swarms of vampirish females would descend.

But when she re-entered the room quite a few minutes later—going to the toilet in a tight full-length satin gown was not a swift process—Tyler was still where she'd left him, and only one woman was in attendance. His sister, Cleo.

That they were exchanging angry words was obvi-ous from the dark looks on both their faces. And Cleo's mouth was going fifty to the dozen. But when Michele drew alongside she immediately clammed up and stalked off back to her own yuppie male partner.

'You were arguing about me, weren't you?'

Michele said. 'Your sister doesn't like the idea of our going out together.'

The muscles in Tyler's jaw tightened. 'Something like that.'

Michele frowned. 'She's never liked me. I'm not sure why. Perhaps you should tell her, Tyler, that we aren't really dating, that it's only a pretence for today. She's a woman. She'll understand about pride and things.'

'I have no intention of explaining my actions to Cleo,' he snapped, clearly still annoyed. 'What I do where you're concerned is none of her business!'

'But, Tyler, she's your sister and she loves you. Even I can see that, despite not having any experience of brothers and sisters loving each other.'

Tyler looked taken aback. 'You don't love your brothers?'

Michele sighed. She had two older brothers who still lived at home with their widowed father. They were like the Three Musketeers together, macho blue-collar men, blustering and swaggering their way through life, needing nothing but their beer and their footie and the occasional lay. Sex was the only need they had for women, which meant Michele's presence in their lives wasn't required.

She was sure her father had only married her mother because she'd been pregnant with Bill, her oldest brother. Michele had never seen her father give her mother one scrap of real affection during their years together. Not a kind word, either. The moment Michele's mother died it had been as though she'd never existed, her father going right back to his old way of life.

Not that he'd ever really left it. He was what some people called 'a man's man', and Bill and Bob were chips off the old block.

Michele shrugged off Tyler's question. She didn't really want to talk about her family. 'Let's just say they don't give me the chance. They simply don't want to know me.'

'But why ever not?'

'It's a long story, Tyler. I'll tell you another time.'

'I'll keep you to that,' he said, so firmly that Michele shot him a startled glance. But she was pleased all the same, pleased that he would want to know. Kevin had never wanted to know anything about her family. Family meant nothing to Kevin.

Family *did* mean something to Michele. The trouble was her feelings in that regard weren't reciprocated.

Maybe that was why she'd clung onto Kevin for so long. Because he'd been her substitute family. And maybe that was why she'd been so susceptible to his flattery and compliments. Because she'd never heard the like from her father or brothers.

'You're really a complex person, aren't you?' Tyler said thoughtfully.

Michele smiled a wry smile. 'Unlike you, you mean?'

'I'm more complex than I look. But that's an even longer story,' he added, smiling just as wryly back.

'Tell me about it,' she quipped.

'I just might do that some time. But for now I think

it's time we found our seats in the dining room across the way. If I'm not mistaken, the wedding feast is about to begin.'

Michele could not believe her bad luck when their place cards seated them on the same table as Tyler's sister, with Michele right next to one of the men who'd been trying to chat her up. She could have kissed Tyler when he sat down in her seat, letting her sit in his, placing her alongside an older and less offensive chap.

She still found it a difficult couple of hours, trying to eat what she had no appetite for, listening to the sickening speeches, then having to toast the happy couple's future. She got through the evening by drinking far too much of the expensive Chardonnay supplied and pretending she didn't give a damn that the man she'd once lived for had thrown her over and married another woman. No one would have guessed that she wasn't totally infatuated with Tyler, given the amount of time she spent with her head bent his way, seemingly whispering sweet nothings in his ear.

In reality, she was making the most impolite cracks about simply everything. By the time they reached dessert Michele was totally sloshed, and incapable of appreciating the exquisitely presented profiteroles, let alone eating them. Fortunately, Tyler had no such reservations, and downed hers as well as his own.

She watched him with a type of tipsy awe.

'I envy you,' she said in slurred tones. 'You can eat anything you want. And you can *have* anyone you want.'

Slowly he placed his fork back down on his plate

and turned his head till their eyes met, barely inches away. 'Can I indeed?' he said with silky smoothness. 'And could I have you, if I wanted you?'

If she hadn't been so drunk, she might have laughed. Or cried.

Instead, she smiled a dangerously reckless smile and lifted a finger to press flirtatiously against his mouth. 'Probably,' she murmured. 'But don't tell Kevin.'

He just stared at her, then slowly took her finger and placed it back in her lap. 'You're drunk,' he said quietly. 'So I'll forgive you for that. But I really wouldn't take your pretence with me too far tonight, Michele, or I might end up doing something we'll both regret in the morning. Now, I must go to the Gents. I suggest you have some coffee in the meantime, since the dancing is about to start and I value my toes.'

Tyler stood up and strode from the room, leaving Michele to drown in mortification. She downed two swift cups of coffee in a valiant effort to sober up and not make any more of a fool of herself than she already had. It was a relief when the music started and the rest of the table stood up to dance, including Cleo and her partner, leaving her to wallow in her misery in peace.

Kevin's suddenly sitting down in Tyler's empty seat was such a shock Michele almost spilled her coffee.

'I've only got a few moments,' he said, 'so I'll be quick. I know I hurt you by not telling you in advance about my marriage, and I'm truly sorry. I meant to the last time we met but I simply couldn't. I knew you still loved me, you see, and I...well, I simply couldn't bear to see the pain in your eyes.'

He gave her the most imploring look, as though waiting for her forgiveness once more. When it wasn't forthcoming, he sighed. 'It wasn't me who sent you the invitation. It was Danni. She wanted to make sure our relationship was really over. On both sides. But to be honest I was relieved when it seemed you weren't coming. I knew you weren't over anything. That's why I was so shocked to see you with Tyler. Which brings me to the point of this little chat...'

His face grew very serious and concerned, his voice low and warm and seemingly sincere. 'I'm worried about you going out with Tyler. He eats girls like you for breakfast. Once he's had you every which way he can, he'll toss you over for a new model. The longest he's ever gone out with a girl is a few weeks. And they were stunners! Frankly, I'm surprised he asked you out at all, unless it was because you represented a challenge. You never did gush all over him like other women...

'Till now, that is,' he added somewhat bitterly. 'I've been watching you with him all night, and frankly, Michele, I thought you had more sense. Oh, I dare say he's great in bed, but don't start winding romantic dreams around him. And for pity's sake don't fall in love with him. Men like Tyler don't marry girls like you. If and when they marry, they pick trophy wives, really classy beautiful women, with fantastic bodies and—'

'I get the picture, Kevin,' she broke in sharply. 'I'm

not the fool I used to be. I know full well what kind of man Tyler is. And I know full well what kind of man *you* are. Now, go back to your rich bitch wife and leave me alone. After today I never want to see you again, as long as I live!'

His eyes narrowed on her. 'Your anger's a dead giveaway, sweetheart,' he muttered. 'Hell, I should have realised. You're only sleeping with Tyler to spite me. That's why you came here with him today, too. Out of spite!'

She opened her mouth to deny everything, but no words came out.

'Best of luck,' Kevin muttered as he stood up. 'Believe me, you're going to need it.'

A pale-faced Michele just sat there watching him go back to the bridal table, where he gave his bride a long and loving kiss.

'What was that all about?'

Michele jerked her head up to find Tyler standing there.

'Nothing,' she choked out.

'In that case, *nothing* has affected you rather badly. Come on, I've had enough of this. I'm taking you home.'

She didn't protest when he levered her to her feet, nor when they didn't stop to say goodbye to anyone.

Tears welled up in her eyes on their way down the stairs.

'I hate him,' she sniffled once they reached Tyler's car.

'Good,' Tyler said, and swept open the passenger

door. 'Now, duck your head and get in. There are tissues in the glove box. I bought them with this moment in mind.'

She practically fell into the car, where she fumbled open the glove box. By the time Tyler climbed in behind the wheel her face was buried in a wad of them.

'I...I don't deserve a f...friend like you,' she blubbered.

'Probably not,' Tyler agreed. 'But you've got me anyway. Better fasten your seat belt.'

She stopped blowing her nose to throw him a panicky glance. 'You haven't had too much to drink, have you?'

'Not even remotely. You didn't leave me any.'

'I'm not *that* drunk!'

'Honey, you're plastered. If I wanted to have my wicked way with you, you wouldn't stand a chance.'

Tyler's words sobered her up much more quickly than any coffee, bringing with them that old irritation she knew so well. 'Well, we don't have to worry about that, do we?' she huffed. 'I'm the last female on earth you'd want to have your wicked way with, since you'd regret it so bitterly in the morning.'

'Only tomorrow morning. I didn't say I'd regret it any other morning.'

'Huh?'

'Look, I might be a sexual predator at times, but I don't need to seduce a girl when she's in her cups and broken-hearted as well.'

'I'm not broken-hearted,' she denied. Just sick at

heart. And full of self-disgust. Tyler was right. Only a masochist could have loved that creep for so long!

'Yeah. Right.'

'And I'm not that drunk.' Well, maybe she was.

'No kidding?'

'And I *want* you to have your wicked way with me,' she heard herself saying, then compounded her stupidity by adding, 'Not some other night, either. Tonight!'

CHAPTER SIX

MICHELE regretted the words the moment they were out of her mouth.

How could she have belittled herself so much as to ask a man to sleep with her when he obviously didn't want to?

It was all Lucille's fault for putting the silly idea in her head in the first place!

No, no, it was all Tyler's fault, she decided angrily, for being impossibly beautiful and sexy and downright irresistible!

And of course she *was* drunk. No doubt about it. No point in denying it any longer.

Finally, she dared to glance over at Tyler, who was looking at her as though she'd grown horns and a tail.

'Sorry,' she muttered. 'Didn't mean to embarrass or shock you. You're right. I'm plastered. Don't know what I'm saying.'

He shook his head at her. 'If I thought you did, I'd...I'd...'

'You'd what?' she challenged, at Tyler's most uncustomary stammer.

His lips pressed hard together in definite annoyance. 'We'll discuss this later,' he bit out. '*After* you've sobered up a bit.'

'Later?' she squawked. 'You mean you're coming back up to the flat with me?'

'Any reason I shouldn't? It's only ten-thirty…and, as much as the alcohol has propelled you into a sudden hormone overload, you're not going to rip my clothes off and ravish me, are you?'

'Er…I guess not.' Though, damn it all, the idea had its attractions. She must be even drunker than she felt!

'Under the circumstances, I'd like to see you safely inside and tucked into bed before I leave.'

Michele closed her eyes and prayed for salvation, but her mind just went from bad to worse!

'You're not feeling sick, are you?'

Her eyes flickered back open. 'No,' she said wearily, almost wishing she was. Anything would be better than this reckless heat which was coursing through her veins, not to mention the R-rated video which kept playing in her head.

'If you feel ill during the drive home,' Tyler warned, 'just yell out and I'll stop. I'm well experienced in driving drunks home.'

Michele refrained from asking if he meant of the male or female variety. 'I'll do that,' she muttered. 'Just drive, will you?'

She was glad when he did as ordered and just drove. She didn't want to talk to him any more, or look at him any more, or crave him any more.

With a groan, she closed her eyes again and tipped her head back against the leather seat, willing herself into a sensible frame of mind, at the same time attempting to banish any further wild sexual impulses to that area reserved for fantasies. Because that was what Tyler was. A fantasy. A sexual fantasy. A most exciting but very unwise sexual fantasy.

The drive home was much too short. Michele had neither sobered up enough nor found total composure by the time Tyler zapped into one of the guest car spaces under her building.

'Got your keycard with you?' he asked as he helped her out. 'You'll need it to get through that door, remember?'

'What? Oh, oh, yes…' She retrieved her purse from the floor and together they made their way through the basement security door and up the two flights of stairs. Once again Tyler put a gallant hand on her elbow, and this time Michele had to force herself not to make a fuss. Not because of any independent feminist stance, but because she was suddenly shockingly aware of Tyler's touch, the heat of his palm and the closeness of his body by her side.

By the time she opened her front door and moved inside she could not get away from him fast enough, making the first excuse she could think of. 'Would you mind if I left you alone out here while I shower and change?' she blurted out. 'I really can't stand this outfit any longer. It might look good, but it's darned uncomfortable.'

'Go right ahead,' he said equably. 'Do *you* mind if I make myself some coffee in the meantime? I missed out on mine back there.'

'Make yourself right at home,' she said, then dashed for the bathroom.

Michele had stripped off and dived into the shower before she realised her mistake. In her haste she'd forgotten to bring a change of clothes with her. The bathroom wasn't of the *en suite* kind, coming off her bedroom, but opened straight into the living room, where Tyler would be sitting. No way was she going to go out there wrapped only in a towel.

She glanced around the steam-filled room, looking for something else to put on, relieved when she spied the towelling robe hooked over a peg by the door. It was cream, one of those one-size-fits-all robes that hotels specialised in and which Kevin had left behind. Michele had washed it, then hung it up there because she'd expected Kevin back one day.

More fool her!

Still, it was big enough and thick enough and sexless enough to provide the perfect security blanket to cocoon herself in before emerging to face Tyler once more.

Feeling much happier, she lifted her face to the warm spray and let it begin the task of washing her make-up down the drain—and her sexy hairdo with it. Fifteen minutes later, the reflection in the mirror was very reassuring. Now *there* was a girl only an ordinary man would fancy! Certainly not a drop-dead gorgeous playboy used to the most stunning creatures God ever put breath into!

Michele felt much more comfortable with her face all pink and scrubbed, her brown eyes *au naturel* and her hair dripping onto her shoulders.

Picking up a fresh towel, she left the room, vigorously rubbing the wet ends and affecting a nonchalant air. Tyler had turned on the television set and was leaning back in the chair by the window, his hands cupped around a steaming mug of no doubt very sweet coffee.

He glanced up at her entry, his handsome face wearing an equally nonchalant expression. Though his wasn't at all feigned. Tyler was back to being Tyler once more. Totally relaxed. Superbly assured. And depressingly indifferent to how she looked.

'Feel better now?' he asked.

'Much,' she returned through faintly gritted teeth. He didn't care in the slightest that she was naked beneath the robe. 'Anything on TV?'

'I don't know. I wasn't really watching it. I was thinking.'

'About what?'

'About having my wicked way with you,' he said. 'Do you still want me to?'

All the breath rushed from her lungs, her lips parting as her heart went into temporary cardiac arrest.

'Ah,' he said, nodding. 'I see by the look on your face that you've sobered up somewhat and don't want my services any more, either for bed tucking in or bed sharing.' He put down his coffee and rose to his feet, his hands lifting to scrape rather wearily through his till then slicked back hair, the action leaving a longish lock flopped over his forehead. It looked rather Great Gatsbyish, and reminded her of the first day she'd seen him, looking incredibly glamorous and rakish.

Michele could only stare at him, still not breathing.

'I rather suspected that might be the case,' he went on, flicking sardonic eyes her way again. 'Just as well, perhaps, because if you'd said yes I'm not sure I would have been able to resist. Still, I'd best be going. You look too deliciously tempting in that bathrobe for me to continue being noble indefinitely. Goodnight, Michele. I'll give you a ring some time shortly and we'll go out for lunch. Or dinner, if you dare. I won't walk over there and give you a goodnight peck. Trust me when I say keeping my distance from you at this moment is the wisest course of action.'

He began striding for the door, male perfection on two legs.

And she was letting him get away! In another few seconds he would be gone, this magnificent man who'd just called *her* deliciously tempting and who didn't seem to mind her hair wet and messy. Kevin had always said she looked like a half-drowned cat with her hair washed.

'Wait!' she called out, and Tyler halted mid-stride.

Michele scooped in some much-needed air before going on. Still, her voice came out breathless and husky. 'I...I don't want you to go. I want you to stay.'

He spun slowly round on his heels, his face wary.

'Meaning what?'

'Meaning I...I want you to stay.'

'All night, you mean?'

She hadn't really got that far in her mind. But once the thought was there, it made her head spin. 'Yes,' was all she could manage.

His eyes narrowed. 'You're not talking about me sleeping out here on the sofa, are you?'

'No…'

'Are you still drunk?'

'No!'

'Then why?'

'Why?'

'Yes. Give me three good reasons why you want to sleep with me and you're on. But let me warn you, if any of them are to do with Kevin's wedding today then I'm out of here like a shot.'

'That's not fair! How can I separate what I feel tonight with what happened today?'

'Try.'

'Look, I'm as surprised as you are,' she blurted out. 'All I know is that ever since you kissed me I've been wanting your arms around me again. I want you to kiss me again. And I want to see if…if…' A flustering heat zoomed into her cheeks.

'Go on,' he insisted. 'Tell the truth and shame the devil!'

'All right!' she snapped. 'I want to know if you're as good at sex as you are at everything else!'

She'd startled him. That was for sure. His eyes flared wide and for once in his life he was speechless.

Michele took advantage of his tongue-tied state to satisfy her own inner need for some truth. 'Now I'd like to know why you would want to sleep with me,' she countered. 'You've never found me "deliciously tempting" before. Give *me* three good reasons why you want to tonight. And if any of them are to do with

Kevin's wedding then you certainly will be out of here like a shot. I'll throw you out myself!'

His laugh showed he'd recovered from his earlier shock, though he still didn't sound too happy. 'You really make a guy pay for the privilege, don't you? What is it that you expect, Michele? A declaration of love?'

'Don't be ridiculous. I want the truth, thanks. I'd never believe such a stupid thing, anyway,' she scorned. The very idea!

'No. I dare say you wouldn't.'

'Well? Cat got your tongue? Or can't you think of any reason other than this is your being-kind-to-Michele day, when any sacrifice isn't too great for the poor heartbroken little thing?'

He laughed. 'God, but you're way out, honey. Way, way out!'

'Spit it out, then.'

'Okay. I want to sleep with you tonight because I've wanted to for quite some time. Ages, in fact...' He walked towards her with a ruthless deliberation, grabbing the hairbrush out of her frozen hand and tossing it carelessly aside. 'I've dreamt about undressing you,' he ground out, his hands untying the sash which anchored the robe around her statue-like body.

'And kissing you all over,' he added thickly, unwrapping the robe and pushing it back off her shoulders.

It pooled at her feet, leaving her standing there in the nude.

Michele was in a state of shock, her breathing instantly fast and shallow, her mind disbelieving of the way his eyes raked over her, so hot and so hungry. Could this be the Tyler she knew, confessing to a long-unrequited desire for her, yet nobly waiting till Kevin was off the scene before he made a move? It didn't make sense, unless it was as Kevin had said, that he found her a challenge because she'd shown no interest in him, a challenge he was now determined to conquer.

Now *that* made sense. Tyler never liked to fail at anything.

'But I've wanted to do this more than anything,' he grated out.

And, scooping her naked body up in his arms, he carried her swiftly through her open bedroom door.

CHAPTER SEVEN

HER BEDROOM was a large room, despite the huge built-in wardrobe which had been added during refurbishment, leaving plenty of space for the queen-sized brass bed which now dominated it.

Not that there was much other furniture. A couple of cream-painted bedside tables, a dressing table in rosewood and one rather well-used green velvet chair.

There were two windows, one opposite the foot of the bed and another smaller one high above the bedhead. Both had sheer cream curtains covering them, through which either moonlight or the city lights were now filtering. Unless the vertical blinds were drawn, the room was never completely dark.

So, despite kicking the door shut behind him, Tyler had no need to turn on any lights to negotiate the room. Without hesitation he strode across the sable-coloured carpet and deposited her in the middle of her daisy-covered duvet.

Michele experienced a weird moment of relief that the bed was not one she'd shared with Kevin. It was a fairly recent purchase, replacing the water bed she'd had for years and which had finally sprung a leak, possibly due to her stabbing it on Kevin's side with a corkscrew after his last departure.

Still, she'd always wanted a brass bed, Kevin having vetoed this wish because he said they squeaked.

She had news for him. Hers didn't.

She had news for Tyler too. She was suddenly panic-stricken at what she was doing.

'Tyler,' she choked out, clutching at the lapels of his jacket and pulling herself back up with him as he tried to climb off the bed. 'Maybe I am drunk after all... I mean I... I...'

'Shh,' he murmured, gently disengaging her hands and lowering her back down onto the pillows before straightening to strip off his jacket and rip off his bowtie, tossing both carelessly aside.

Somehow, they landed on the velvet chair.

She shut her eyes and heard the sound of shoes being kicked off, then the snap of her bedside lamp being switched on. There was only the one, a gold-shaded number with an elegantly curved brass base. The mattress dipped abruptly beside her and two large but soft-palmed hands curved over her bare shoulders. Tyler's expensive cologne wafted up her nostrils.

'Don't close your eyes,' he murmured, his mouth so close to hers that she could feel the warmth of his breath on her lips, and smell the coffee he'd recently drunk. 'You have such beautiful eyes...'

How could she keep them shut after that?

Her eyelids fluttered upwards and there he was in all his golden glory, looming over her, his own truly beautiful blue eyes intent on her face. For which she was rather glad. Whilst not ashamed of her body, it was very difficult for her to lie there naked, especially when he was still clothed.

'Aren't...aren't you getting undressed?' she asked shakily.

'Not yet,' came his soft reply, and he moved to stretch out on his side beside her, still in his white shirt and black trousers. 'Since I'm staying the whole night, there's no reason to rush things, is there?' Leaning over, he propped his elbows on either side of her upper arms before bending to kiss her lips oh, so lightly, over and over, all the while stroking her still damp hair back from her face and staring down into her eyes as though she were the loveliest and most desirable creature in the world.

'You've no idea how often I've thought of doing this,' he confessed.

Any nerves receded as Michele became bewitched by his tender and seemingly sincere desire. She no longer cared if she did only represent a sexual challenge to him, as long as he kept kissing her like this and looking at her like this. He was making her feel so beautiful, and wanted, and special, which was what she so desperately needed to feel that night.

Her lungs expelled a long-held breath and she surrendered herself totally to the moment.

'That's good,' he murmured against her melting mouth. 'Relax...' He trailed light, feathery kisses over her whole face, her chin, her cheeks, her nose, her eyelids, her forehead, before finally going back to her mouth.

But then the tenor of his kisses changed.

Capturing her bottom lip between both of his, he tugged at its soft flesh, rubbing it with his tongue and teeth, before releasing it in a slightly swollen and highly sensitised state. Michele's heartbeat quickened once more, then bolted into a full gallop when he repeated the erotic action. By the time he'd done the same to her top lip her mouth felt as if it was on fire.

And so was she.

A soft groan escaped her throat when his kisses changed once more, his hands splaying into her damp hair and gripping her scalp as he took full possession of her lips, then sent his tongue stabbing deep into her mouth.

Michele's head was beginning to whirl when he suddenly yanked his mouth away.

'Sorry,' he muttered, his breathing raw and ragged. 'Got a bit carried away there. Understandable…under the circumstances. But unforgivable all the same.'

Michele had no idea what he was talking about.

Not that she was thinking too clearly at that moment. Tyler's abrupt abandonment of her mouth had focused what little was left of her thought processes on an acute awareness of her own very excited state. Her body burned and yearned in a way quite alien from her experiences with Kevin. She felt driven, not by a desire to please, but a desire to be pleased. And Tyler's mouth on hers had definitely been pleasing her.

'Don't stop,' she rasped, and lifted her head till her mouth brushed against his, her tongue-tip darting out to taste her lips.

He grabbed her shoulders, holding her just far

enough away so that she couldn't do it again. His blue eyes glittered down at her, his mouth twisting wryly. 'Have some pity on me, woman. I'm a man, not a machine.'

'I know,' she whispered. 'The most beautiful man I've ever seen.'

His face darkened, and he released her so abruptly that she flopped back onto the pillows. 'What's beauty when all's said and done?' he grated out. 'It's just an illusion. And sometimes a curse.'

'I'd like to be beautiful.'

'Don't be ridiculous. You *are* beautiful. How many times do I have to tell you? You think this isn't beautiful?' he said, sweeping the back of his right hand down over her tautly held nakedness.

When one of his fingernails scraped over a breast, Michele sucked in sharply. Startled by the blindingly electric sensation, she lifted her hands to find that both her nipples were already erect and exquisitely sensitive. She touched them tentatively, wonderingly, never having known them to be so responsive. Or so... needy.

'Don't,' Tyler commanded harshly.

Her head jerked up and she stared at him. His eyes were narrowed on her. Hungry eyes. Tormented eyes. She hardly recognised him.

But then his anguished expression melted away and she saw once again the Tyler she was familiar with. That cool, superbly confident creature who was rarely rattled and simply oozed sexual *savoir faire*.

'Let me,' he said, with suave wickedness.

A dazed Michele was hardly in a position to *let* him do anything.

He didn't wait for her permission, anyway, reaching to grip her offending hands by their wrists and lifting them up, up over her head, the action shifting her breasts higher on her chest wall, taking those needy nipples with them till they were pointing right at where his mouth was inexorably descending.

Michele could only stare in heart-pounding anticipation.

When his lips first made contact, a strangled sound escaped her lips. When he licked the ever-tightening tip, she stopped breathing altogether. When he started sucking on it, she wasn't sure if she could stand the sensations. Her whole body stiffened, her back arching, her lips bursting apart on a feverish gasp.

Quite accidentally, her fingertips brushed against one of the horizontal railings in the bedhead, and instinctively she stretched for it, her fingers curling tightly around the cool brass rod like a drowning man clutching at a straw.

Michele was dimly aware that Tyler's hands no longer imprisoned her wrists, but she stayed as she was, a willing victim on an erotic rack. Her eyes were squeezed tightly shut and she had no idea of how she looked to the man making love to her as he lifted his head from her breast to stare down at her outstretched nudity.

It was, after all, only a few seconds before his mouth returned to claim her other breast, making Michele think he'd only been moving from one nipple to the other. She would never have pictured him clenching his fists at her attitude of mindless rapture, momentarily distressed by the fact that she wanted nothing from him but the assets God had given him and the sexual prowess he'd learned through a decade of seeking physical distraction from his emotional pain.

Michele was oblivious of everything but the dark excitement possessing her as she was propelled from one mind-blowing experience to the next. Never had she felt such pleasure, or such sweet torment.

Tyler's hands had by now joined his lips in all sorts of tantalising foreplay, stroking a breast while the other was licked, then suckled, playing with its still wet peak, rolling it and pinching it till she was whimpering softly. Only when she felt that hand leave her breast to stroke down over her tensely held stomach did her eyes fly open, widening further when she watched his broad fingers slide down into the desire-dampened curls between her legs, immediately zeroing in on that exquisitely sensitive spot which Kevin had often been indifferent to finding.

She gasped with delight at Tyler's knowing touch, then with shock when he deserted her breasts entirely to slide down and attempt to put his mouth where his fingertips had been.

'No, no!' she immediately cried, squirming and twisting away from him.

Tyler sat back up with surprise on his face. 'You don't like that?'

'I... I...well, I don't really know,' she stammered,

feeling suddenly embarrassed and grabbing for the edge of the duvet, pulling it over her lower half. 'I mean... Kevin never... He didn't... He didn't like doing that,' she finished with an almost defiant stance, dragging the duvet further up over her still throbbing breasts.

Of course, what she'd said was a huge understatement. Kevin had *hated* doing it. Hadn't even entertained the idea after one pathetic attempt. He'd claimed he hated the taste of a woman down there. Hated the position he had to adopt. Hated everything about it.

Michele had developed a huge hang-up about it, except in her fantasies. In her fantasies she would lie wantonly back with her legs wide open and some beast-like male feeding ravenously upon her while she came and came and came. She'd even fantasised about Tyler doing it earlier today. But a fantasy was just that. A fantasy. Reality was very different.

'Well, I'm not Kevin,' Tyler said drily as he stood up and began to undo the buttons on his shirt. 'And I happen to like it a lot. I think you might like it too...if you let yourself. What say you just trust me to do what comes naturally? And if I do anything you don't like—anything at all—just say so, and I'll stop immediately. Fair enough?'

Michele nodded, then watched, wide-eyed, while he stripped to the waist, revealing some of the body which had made women go weak at the knees for years. She knew Tyler worked out regularly, but no amount of weights could change the framework on which his well-honed muscles were built.

And Tyler's framework was superb. Broad shoulders and chest, narrow waist. Slim hips. Tight butt. Long, strong legs and arms. There was nothing wrong with his skin, either. Satin-smooth, almost hair-free. And the most gloriously golden-brown colour.

Michele couldn't wait to touch it, to touch *him*.

By now he was working on his belt, which reminded her of her earlier mistaken assumption about his belt buckle, followed by a stark memory of other things. Her eyes dropped a few inches and there it was, that…other thing.

She stared at the obvious bulge in his pants.

If oral sex was part of Tyler's normal foreplay then he would surely want her to do it to him as well. The prospect sent nervous flutters churning all through her stomach.

It wasn't that she found the idea repulsive. She really didn't mind doing it.

Her problem was…would Tyler like the way she did it? He'd had so many women and she…well, she'd only been with Kevin, and whilst Kevin had seemed pleased with her technique in that regard, she wasn't sure if he'd really meant it now, or if his compliments had just been flattery.

Tyler's trousers dropped to the floor, then his underpants, swiftly followed by Michele's mouth.

Now she knew why Kevin had always felt inferior to Tyler. And it had nothing to do with his money.

She swallowed, wishing she hadn't sobered up quite

so much. Things had been much easier when she was plastered. Nothing had fazed her then.

Still, she wanted to do it to him really, didn't she? As much as she wanted him to do it to her.

There! She'd told the truth and shamed the devil once more!

Once his underpants were kicked aside, Tyler turned his back and sat down on the edge of the bed, bending to peel off his socks before scooping his trousers back up, where he hunted till he found what he was looking for.

Michele assumed it was a condom. She also assumed he always had one or two with him. Being Tyler, he would never know when he might need one.

Tyler tossed two foil packets onto the bedside chest, then stretched out, totally naked and fully erect, on top of the bed next to her.

Michele didn't know where to look.

'Shall we both get in under the sheets?' he suggested, taking the duvet out of her nerveless fingers and tossing it back over the edge of the bed. 'Or can I persuade you to resume that absolutely incredible position of a few minutes ago?'

Michele blinked. 'You mean...?' And her eyes flicked up over her head at the brass bedhead.

'Uh-huh,' he confirmed.

When she hesitated, he started kissing her again, deep, drugging, dizzying kisses which soon sent any scruples and inhibitions scattering. After five minutes or so she'd have probably hung naked from the chandelier if he'd asked her. If she'd *had* a chandelier, that was.

In the end she didn't have to actually adopt the provocative position herself. Tyler seductively stroked her arms back up over her head between kisses and placed her palms right where he wanted them, even curling her hands over the brass rod for her.

'Promise me you won't let go,' he whispered in her ear while he ran his fingertips up and down the soft skin of her upper arms. 'Not till I tell you to...'

A nod was all she could manage. Already she was beside herself with the most intoxicating mixture of excitement and anticipation, every muscle in her erotically outstretched body quivering with tension.

'You can close your eyes, if you want to.'

She *did* want to, yet when she did her mind was instantly awash with doubts and fears. What exactly was he going to do to her? Would she like it or hate it? Maybe she'd still cringe away in embarrassment. Maybe she'd...

All mental arguings ceased when his hands moved from her upper arms in a journey downwards, dipping into her armpits, grazing over her breasts and her stomach before moving sidewards to her hips, then down onto her thighs. There they lingered, for what was probably only a few seconds but felt like an eternity. Did he part her legs or did she part them for him? Afterwards, Michele would never be sure, and by then it wouldn't really matter. Whatever, they found themselves apart, and she was holding her breath, waiting for him to put his lips there, waiting for the unknown to become known.

How to describe it? How to capture in words the variety and complexity of the pleasure he gave her? Was it just physical, or was there some other deeply emotional need being satisfied by him that night? Impossible to gauge in hindsight. All Michele knew was that he did everything she'd ever dreamt about and fantasised over. And he did it all with a primitive and primal passion which bypassed embarrassment and brought out the female animal in her. Under his mouth and hands she wasn't the Michele she'd become with Kevin—a nervous try-hard—but a wild bitch in heat, driven by uncontrollable hormones and the most basic of instincts, to mate and be mated with.

She writhed and she whimpered, moaning and groaning, crying out in her arousal and abandonment. She came as she'd fantasied, with his mouth clamped to her flesh and his fingers deep inside. Then again as he licked her all over afterwards. Then again when he teased her some more with a slow and wickedly knowing hand.

Yet surprisingly, by the time he deserted her to reach for a condom, she wasn't in any way sated, her body still as strung up as it had been before he started. She literally ached for his penetration, knowing that then and only then would she feel satisfied, with his flesh filling hers and his own desire finally released deep within her body.

Her tension mounted when he moved over her, his body poised.

'Yes,' she urged, her dilated eyes smouldering up at him. 'Oh, yes, Tyler, yes!'

He hesitated a moment, then entered her with a single powerful thrust.

A gasp tore from her throat, her fingers clutching at the bedhead as her hips jerked up from the bed.

Tyler groaned, then reached up to take her numbed hands away and wrap them around his back. 'Now you can move all you like,' he commanded, his voice low and thick.

'You too,' she choked back, lifting her knees and wrapping her legs around his waist.

'Yes, ma'am.'

Her body literally rocked with his powerful rhythm, so that she had to cling to him. It was a surprisingly comfortable position, and soon she no longer felt an entity in herself but half of a perfect whole, their flesh fused as one, their hearts beating together.

'Oh, Tyler…Tyler… I'm going to come. I can't stop myself.'

'It's all right, baby,' he rasped as his body began to shudder within her own wildly spasming flesh. 'I'm right there…with you.'

CHAPTER EIGHT

'WAKEY, wakey, sleepyhead!'

Michele buried herself even deeper under the duvet, hugging it around her shoulders and simply refusing to budge. She felt too deliciously warm to wake up, still half comatose within her sleepy cocoon.

'Go away, Tyler,' she mumbled into the bedclothes, before a jolt penetrated the mist enveloping her brain.

Tyler?

All mental fogginess vanished when the memory of the night before suddenly flashed onto the screen of her mind in full Vista Vision, complete with Dolby sound. Everything she'd done was there to instantly relive, every humiliating word—and moan—she'd uttered.

'It's almost midday,' Tyler said from somewhere awfully close. 'Come on, sexy.' He actually dropped a kiss on the top of her rumpled head. 'The day awaits us.'

Now she definitely wanted to crawl right under the duvet and never surface again. She squeezed her eyes tightly shut and prayed for salvation. But this wasn't a movie and the cavalry wasn't going to arrive at the last minute to rescue her. She had to face the music.

One eyelid flicked open warily, only to land not on Tyler, who was standing behind her turned back, but on the three empty foil packets still sitting under the lamp on the bedside chest.

Three. Not two.

Michele gnawed at her bottom lip, only to find it puffy and bruised. Tentatively she felt her nipples, and they too were still sore and highly sensitive to the touch.

So she hadn't imagined *any* of it. None of the erotic torment Tyler had subjected her to. Nor that second amazing time, when he'd manoeuvred her into a position which had driven her simply crazy. Or her hunting high and low to find the third condom some time in the middle of the night, after he'd rolled over and started making love to her yet again and she simply hadn't been able to resist.

And whilst it had all been madly exciting at the time, in the cold light of morning Michele's main feeling was mortification. How could she have let Tyler do all those things to her? It wasn't as though she loved him. Or vice versa. It had been nothing but sex in its most basic and primitive form. Lust, not love.

And yet…it had been incredible!

Michele suppressed a groan. She'd always thought she was a girl who needed love to enjoy sex.

Oh, yeah? And how long is it since you enjoyed sex like that with Kevin, sweetheart?

So long ago she could hardly remember. Maybe never!

'Come along. No more pretending to be still asleep,' Tyler ordered, with more than a hint of knowingness in his voice. 'I do realise you might be having problems with the morning-after syndrome, but I can assure you it's totally wasted. I doubt Kevin's lying in his honeymoon suite bed at this moment either regretting the night before or giving you a second thought.'

Michele lay there for a few moments, pondering Tyler's potentially provocative words with a degree of surprise. For there simply wasn't any pain in her heart over them. No pain at all.

On top of that amazing realisation rested the equally amazing fact that she hadn't been thinking of Kevin at all, except in as far as he was a very ordinary lover when compared with Tyler. In all honesty, she didn't give a damn what Kevin was thinking or not thinking that morning. All she seemed to care about at that moment was finding the courage to face Tyler and find out what *he* was thinking. Because, quite frankly, she had no idea!

Swallowing, she rolled over, pushed the hair out of her face at the same time and adopted what she hoped was a suitably thoughtful expression. But the sight of him standing there, wrapped in Kevin's cream bathrobe, looking like some golden Greek god just stepped out of an opulent Turkish bath, scattered her brainwaves.

She kept looking at his mouth and his hands, and thinking of the beautiful and wonderfully virile naked body which lay beneath that bathrobe, that body which she'd always admired but which she now knew very, very intimately. She thought of how, that third time, she'd touched him all over, and kissed him all over, and, yes, done *that* to him too…if only for a few brief moments. He hadn't let her go all the way, however, but had hauled her up on top of him and urged her to ride him till she came, before rolling her underneath and pounding into her till he climaxed as well.

It had been after that that she'd fallen into an exhausted and satiated sleep.

But now she was wide awake. And she wasn't exhausted any longer. She wasn't satiated, either.

Shock at her train of thought sent her stomach contracting and dismay into her eyes. She wasn't sure if she wanted to be this new lustful creature Tyler had created.

Michele had always been an obsessive person, but the last thing she wanted to become obsessive about was sex, or Tyler. She better than anyone knew what he was like where females were concerned. Hadn't she watched him from the sidelines for ten years? His girlfriends came, then went, perhaps because they came. Too easily and too often. Like a lot of highly intelligent men, Tyler had a low boredom threshold. He needed challenges and goals to keep up his interest in a project, or a person. He enjoyed succeeding where others had failed, such as with his magazine.

Michele recalled his confession last night that he'd wanted to sleep with her for ages. She'd been pretty flattered at the time. Common sense now suggested that it had nothing to do with her having lovely eyes— or a beautiful body—but was because she'd always ignored him that way, just as Kevin had said. She'd become the ultimate sexual challenge for Tyler, the one girl who hadn't been prepared to throw herself at his head, and his feet.

Till last night…

Chagrin joined other upsetting emotions. She didn't like the thought of just being another notch on Tyler's sexual gun. She didn't like it at all!

'Oh-oh,' Tyler said drily.

'Oh-oh, *what*?' she snapped.

'You're warming yourself up for a fight. I can see it in your eyes. But you won't get one from me, honey. Not this time. I'm going to be so agreeable today that you won't have anything to get your teeth into. I'm going to say yes to whatever you say and whatever you want.' He flopped down on top of the bed beside her and stretched out, ankles crossing, his arms going up behind his head. 'I'm yours to command. Totally.'

Michele wanted to be angry with him. But it was impossible.

Besides, a temper tantrum took both time and energy, and she was too busy fighting off the most incredibly wicked temptations. Hard enough finding the will to drag her eyes away from his outstretched body. His hair was still damp, which meant he'd recently showered, so his freshly washed flesh was just lying there, waiting for her to take up where she'd left off the night before. In her mind's eyes she was already undoing that sash and peeling the robe back, running her hands all over his beautiful bare chest and bending to kiss his rock-hard stomach, then to…

'You're right!' she choked out with false brightness. 'Time I was up!'

She was already sitting up and throwing back her side of the duvet before she realised her mistake. But by then it was too late to grab the darned thing back again and hide her nakedness from Tyler's eyes. Thank the Lord she had her back to him.

Rising to her feet with as much dignity as she could muster, she covered the distance between herself and the wardrobe doors with agonisingly casual steps. To bolt would have been demeaning.

But presenting a naked back to him proved as hazardous as full-frontal nudity. She kept thinking of him lying there, staring at her bare buttocks and remembering himself pressed up hard against them as he pumped into her, his hot words sending her spiralling out into a dark, erotic world she'd never known before.

Hold onto me tight, honey. Don't let me go... Oh, yes, baby, yes... That's the way... You do the moving now... Oh, yes... That's it... Don't stop... Don't stop...

Her hand trembled as it reached for her own dressing gown—a roomy purple number with buttons down the front but no sash. Michele resisted diving into it like the shaken and highly vulnerable marshmallow she suddenly was, sliding it over her nudity with what she hoped was the right amount of nonchalance.

'I think I'll go have a shower,' she told Tyler with a flicked glance over her shoulder.

'Want me to make you some coffee while you do that?' he offered, before she could escape the room.

She stopped in the doorway and turned to face him once more. He'd swung his feet over the side of the bed and was sitting there, watching her intently, his eyes both thoughtful and curious. Michele's pretend confidence faltered badly and she clutched at the door-frame. Oh, God, what was he thinking now? What was he remembering? Or wanting? Or expecting?

'No, don't worry,' she said tautly. 'I'll get myself some when I'm finished in the bathroom.'

'Running away won't help, you know,' he said quietly. 'It happened, Michele. And it was great.'

Michele stiffened, then decided to ignore that last statement. Denying that the sex was great was futile. But confirming it was not an option. Tyler's ego didn't need any more stroking.

'I'm well aware of what happened,' she flung at him. 'And I'm not running away. I'm merely going to have a shower.'

'And afterwards?'

'I'll have some breakfast.'

'And then?'

'Then you can get dressed and go home. After which, hopefully, we can both go back to where we were before yesterday.'

His laughter scraped over raw nerves. 'Which was where, exactly?' he demanded to know, some anger in his voice now. 'Pretending to be friends? Bickering all the time? Trying to ignore the chemistry that's always been there sparking between us?'

Michele was taken aback for a moment. But when she gave his theory due consideration she conceded he was partially right. She'd always been aware of his sex appeal. What female wasn't? And, yes, there might have been a degree of sexual jealousy behind some of the insults she used to throw at him.

'Last night proved me right,' he went on, before she could say a word. 'You wanted me, Michele. And I wanted you. I've always wanted you. I told you so and I meant it!'

'Why?' she challenged, needing to hear the truth.

He shrugged. 'Who knows the mystery behind the attraction of the sexes? I've always found you incredibly sexy. And I was right,' he added, smiling suddenly as he stood up and strode towards her. 'You are.'

'I...I'm not usually,' she denied, her heart racing.

'You are with me...' He took her by the shoulders and when she looked up with wide eyes he bent to kiss her upturned mouth.

Michele trembled against his lips and felt the heat of desire zing instantly through her veins.

He was right. She was. With him.

'We can't go back to where we were, Michele,' he said between kisses. 'Last night wasn't a one-night stand, and I won't let you turn it into one.'

'No,' she finally agreed in a dazed voice.

'I want to keep on seeing you. I want to take you out to dinner and dancing, and to the theatre, and, yes, to bed some more. I want to put some fun back into your life.'

'Fun?' she repeated blankly.

'Yes. Do you remember what that is?'

'I... I...'

'I don't wonder you don't,' he drawled. 'Kevin's

sucked all the joy out of you, girl. I aim to put some fun back into you or my name's not Tyler Garrison!'

Michele stared up at him. She supposed it could be fun, dating Tyler, provided you didn't get emotionally involved with him. For, as night followed day, the sun would inevitably set on any relationship she had with him. That was the big catch behind his promise of pleasure, and fun, and joy. Being his girlfriend was always a temporary state of affairs.

'Starting today,' he added firmly.

'What are we going to do today?' she asked, far too breathlessly.

His returning smile was wicked. 'That's for me to know, and you to find out!'

CHAPTER NINE

'YOU DIDN'T!' Lucille exclaimed.

Michele sighed. 'I did.'

It was Monday, and Michele had rung and begged Lucille to meet her somewhere for lunch. She needed a sane, sensible person to talk to, someone who would help keep her feet firmly on the ground—a difficult thing to do when a man like Tyler wanted you to be his next girlfriend.

'I warned you that the big bad wolf would seduce you,' Lucille reminded her scathingly.

'He didn't. I asked him to stay.'

'You *didn't*!'

'I did.'

'I don't believe you. That's not you at all. You're just protecting him, which is *just* like you.'

'Well, I was a wee bit plastered at the time,' Michele confessed.

'I'd say you were a *lot* plastered, and he took disgusting advantage of you.'

'Actually, no, he didn't, Lucille, though I gave him every opportunity to. He was all for tucking me up in bed and leaving me to my misery.'

Lucille laughed. 'You mean that's what he *let* you think. He knew he was onto a sure thing from the moment you asked him to take you to that wedding.

You don't think he asked you to wear something sexy for Kevin's sake, do you?'

Michele's head whirled as Lucille put another new slant on what had happened. 'I don't know, Lucille. Frankly, I don't know anything any more. I mean…when I first woke up yesterday morning I could have just died with humiliation. My God, the things I let him do. And the things I did myself. It's a wonder my hair hadn't turned curly overnight!'

'Ooh, do tell. What *did* you do, exactly?'

Michele shuddered. 'I can't possibly tell you.'

'Of course you can. I'm a woman. Now give!'

Michele told her. Everything. And, to give Lucille credit, she didn't look too scandalised.

'He sounds pretty fantastic in bed,' she whispered across the table, so that the old biddies on the table next to them didn't overhear. They certainly seemed to have stopped drinking their tea during the last few minutes.

'Mind-blowing. When he starts on at me I can't even think, let alone make a rational decision. It's like some stranger takes possession of me and all I want is to lose myself completely in the experience. Sometimes I feel like I want to eat him alive, or draw him so deep into my body that we truly do become one person.'

For the first time Lucille look worried. 'I don't like the sound of that. You haven't fallen for the devil, have you?'

'No…' Michele said, a fraction unconvincingly.

'No, I don't think so. I'm just a bit...blown away. I guess it's not every day that you get made endless love to by a man who knows all the moves and has the equipment to back them up.'

Lucille's eyebrows lifted. 'Really? You hadn't mentioned that part of him. Do tell me more.'

Michele laughed. 'I think I've said enough. You're not being nearly as much help as I'd hoped you'd be. I thought you'd tell me to stop being such a fool, and not to go out with him ever again!'

'I would if I thought you'd take any notice of me,' Lucille said drily. 'But we both know you're going to keep going out with him till he dumps you. And we both know you're going to get hurt again, maybe even more than Kevin hurt you. Because Tyler Garrison is not a man easily forgotten by the sounds of things. Which reminds me? How *do* you feel about Kevin now?'

'Kevin who?'

'Oh, *God*!'

'Just joking, Lucille. You don't forget ten years of your life that easily. Still, I'm done with him for good,' Michele pronounced firmly.

'I hope so. But I seem to recall you said that once or twice before.'

'I mean it this time.'

'That's because you have the gorgeous Tyler as a distraction. What would happen, I wonder, if Kevin left his wife and showed up again?'

Michele wasn't capable of responding to such speculation. Her mind was full of the present and the immediate past, when Tyler had staggered out of her bed early this morning, claiming he would be useless at work today.

'You've done me in, woman,' he'd complained.

'So what did you do for the rest of the weekend?' Lucille asked, and Michele coloured.

'You *didn't*!' Lucille exclaimed again.

'Well, not quite. We did get up and eat occasionally. And we watched a bit of TV. And we talked.'

'Oh, yes?' Lucille murmured, cocking a single cynical brow at her. 'What about? The missing positions in the *Kama Sutra*?'

'My family. Tyler said he wanted to know everything that made me tick.'

'Ooh. Clever, that. There's nothing more attractive than a man capable of asking a woman questions about herself. Makes for a real change. But the object's the same. Keeping them sweet for some more sex.'

Lucille's caustic remarks weren't far off the mark, and reminded Michele of what Kevin had said. that when Tyler had had her every which way he would dump her.

Her mind flashed to this morning, when Tyler had been saying his goodbyes. He'd told her he had a magazine deadline this week and wouldn't be able to see her till Friday night. Had that been just a genuine excuse, or the prelude to his finally saying he didn't want to see her again, period? Was it already almost over?

The hurt was swift and sure, a brutal jab to her heart which was quite physical as well as emotional.

'What is it?' Lucille said. 'What's wrong?'

Michele lifted wounded eyes to her friend.

'Nothing,' she muttered.

But Lucille wasn't fooled. Michele's eyes were the windows to her soul, and simply could not deceive. She was getting involved with that bad, beautiful bastard and Lucille knew it. But what could she do except be there to help pick up the pieces afterwards? Girls like Michele weren't as tough as she was, or as worldly-wise. *She* was capable of conducting a strictly sexual affair. At least…she was sure she *would* be when she found a suitable candidate. But Michele simply wasn't hard enough, or cynical enough, for such cold-blooded pleasures.

Give her time, though…

'Don't let your coffee get cold,' Lucille advised, then changed the subject, at which point the biddies at the next table went back to their lunch with disappointed sighs. Listening to those girls had been better than watching a TV soap.

Michele carried her fear back to work with her that afternoon, and was barely able to concentrate. Yet she really needed to. Her team's presentation of the proposed advertising package for Packard Foods was due at the end of next week. She was more than happy with their progress up to this point, but she didn't need any extra stress and strain in her life between now and then.

'How's things going here, Michele?'

Michele jolted upright in her chair, startled to find her boss standing on the other side of her desk, staring down at her with those steely grey eyes of his.

She tried not to look rattled.

But her boss rattled people very easily.

Harry Wilde was a difficult and demanding man, a workaholic and perfectionist, driven by personal demons which Michele could only guess at. No one knew much about his background, other than what was public knowledge.

In the late eighties he'd been the new young whiz-kid on the advertising executive block, working here in Sydney for a large, flash American-owned company. When he'd been about twenty-five he'd resigned his position there to start up his own company with a staff of one. Him. His office had been a poky one-bedroomed flat in North Sydney and his secretary an answering machine.

The competition hadn't taken him at all seriously for a year or so, calling him a madman, not the brilliant and rather ruthless maverick he really was. The accounts he'd won had been chicken-feed, in their humble opinion. But when he'd signed up a large take-away food chain—selling chicken, not chicken-feed—they'd been forced to sit up and take notice.

By the age of thirty Harry had become a millionaire many times over. By then he'd bought a Porsche and a penthouse in nearby Kirribilli, and his company walked away with several industry awards every year.

Ten years after its inauspicious beginning, Wild Ideas had grown to a staff of fifteen, and now occupied the third floor of an office building in North Sydney, a five-minute drive from Harry's exclusive harbour-side apartment block. Harry didn't believe in wasting time travelling to and from work, which was why he encouraged employees to live locally.

He'd also had the good sense not to plough his money into fancy offices with fancy furniture and fancy views. Whilst his own office and reception rooms were suitably impressive, efficiency and not elegance was the order of the day for the rest of the staff. Michele's own office was a spacious but spartan room, with practical brown carpet and simple pine furniture. Her office and computer equipment, however, was extensive and state-of-the-art.

Harry spared no expense when it came to the latest in PCs, plus all their added paraphernalia. He made sure his staff were happy in the things that really mattered. The people he employed were all dedicated and ambitious people who didn't value plush carpet and three-hour lunches so much as a challenging job, plus the satisfaction and salary which came with success.

Michele schooled her face into what she hoped was a suitably dedicated and ambitious expression.

'Well, actually, Harry,' she began, 'the thing is that—'

She stopped when Harry's right eyebrow arched cynically and his mouth lifted into one of his famous don't-try-to-con-me smiles. It added a dangerous edge to his elegantly handsome face which had Michele swallowing nervously. Harry didn't suffer fools gladly, and his employees would be very foolish if they tried to put anything over on him. He could not abide lame excuses, or wordy explanations. If you were brain dead on occasion, he preferred you to own up to it.

But, brother, that wasn't easy with that piercing gaze boring into her.

'Sorry,' she muttered. 'Can't seem to concentrate today.'

'Anything I can help you with?'

Michele almost smiled. Harry could troubleshoot any advertising problem she might encounter with a speed and brilliance which was breathtaking. But he was the last person on earth she would go to with her personal problems, especially regarding Tyler.

Because, basically, Tyler and Harry were of the same breed. Playboys, both of them. Utterly devoted to the pleasures of the flesh in their leisure time, with no thought whatsoever of true commitment or caring.

Admittedly, Harry didn't devote as much time to leisure as Tyler, but, from what she'd gathered, when he did play, he played hard.

So it was little wonder that Michele didn't voice her doubts about Tyler to her boss. He probably wouldn't even see what her problem was. He'd tell her to go for it, have fun, then have the intelligence to get out before Tyler did!

'I'm just a bit hungover, boss,' she confessed. 'Friend of mine got married at the weekend and there was a right old party afterwards. I'll be back on deck by tomorrow.'

Harry nodded. Being hungover was something he could understand and empathise with. 'Fair enough,' he said. 'But don't go doing anything stupid next weekend. I'm scheduling a full rehearsal of your presentation for first thing next Monday morning. That'll give us time to iron out any kinks.'

Michele stifled a groan. Full rehearsals were a nightmare. Harry always assembled everyone on staff to watch, after which he invited comments and criticisms. Michele had only endured two others since joining Wild Ideas three years ago, because till recently she'd only worked with small accounts, and small accounts rarely warranted such grand measures.

But this was different. This was the big time.

Harry's eyes narrowed. 'You're sure you're on top of things?'

'Positive.'

'You'd better be, sweetheart,' he said drily, then stalked off.

His calling her sweetheart was not unusual and meant nothing.

Which was why Michele started frowning. For it reminded her of the similar nondescript terms of endearment Tyler had called her over the weekend, words such as 'honey', 'baby' and 'darling'. They'd sounded sweet, or even sexy at the time, but in hindsight had probably meant no more than Harry's 'sweetheart'.

How many other girls had Tyler whispered the same endearments to while he screwed them silly?

Michele was trying to hazard a depressing guess when her phone rang. She reached for it irritably, not wanting to talk to anyone right at that moment.

'Yes?' she said, a bit sharply.

'Have I rung at a bad time?'

It was Tyler. Tyler of the seductive voice and the irresistible body.

Michele's hand clenched tighter around the receiver. 'That depends,' she said warily.

'On what?'

'On what you're ringing me about...'

Maybe she wouldn't have to make a decision where he was concerned. Maybe this was the kiss-off call.

Sorry, honey, but I think we'd best leave things at a one-weekend stand. We really don't have anything in common, you know...

Which translated to mean there were much better birds around to bed; girls who wouldn't start coming the heavy with him the morning after, or making him feel guilty because he'd taken advantage of her.

Because Lucille had been right about that. In hindsight, Michele could see Tyler *had* taken advantage of her. He must have known how upset she was over Kevin. And, whether she'd felt drunk or not, she *had* to have been, given the amount of champagne and Chardonnay she'd consumed.

Michele groaned. At least she could cling to both those reasons to explain her uncharacteristically promiscuous and perturbingly impassioned behaviour. She could discard her other much more worrying feelings that maybe Tyler meant more to her than she'd ever imagined.

'About next Friday night,' Tyler began, and Michele stiffened.

'I forgot it's my parents' thirty-fifth wedding anniversary and Cleo's organised a small family dinner party to celebrate.'

How convenient!

Behind the tart thought, however, lay hurt. Far too much hurt. Oh, Michele, you fool!

'And?' she prompted, almost savagely.

'And I just wanted to let you know in advance,' he returned, sounding a little taken aback. 'Thought you might need to buy something new to wear. My mother will be dressed to kill. Cleo, too, I'd imagine. That blue number you wore at the wedding would be just the thing, but I didn't think you'd want to wear that because Cleo just saw you in it. I know what you women are like about such things.'

Michele's blinding joy that he wanted her to come with him was swiftly overshadowed by the prospect of spending an evening trying to compete with his gold-plated mother and snooty sister. She'd spent a bomb on that blue dress and resented having to buy another one.

'Perhaps you should just go alone, Tyler,' she said, trying to sound sensible. But the words came out rather waspishly. 'I mean, Cleo won't be happy with my being there at all, and I'm not so sure your mother would be, either. Call me a reverse snob, if you like, but I only like going where I'm welcome.'

The silence on the other end of the phone was ominous.

'Tyler?'

'I will say this only once more, Michele,' he grated out. 'I don't give a flying fruitfly what Cleo thinks. As for my mother, let me assure you that whatever you're thinking about her is dead wrong. She was an ordinary working-class girl from an ordinary working-class family before she married my father. She will not look down her nose at you. I promise you that.'

Michele could have pointed out his use of the word, *was*. His mother might have been an ordinary working-class girl once, but thirty-five years married to a very rich and powerful man had changed her somewhat. Michele hadn't actually spoken to the woman, true. But she'd been introduced briefly at Tyler's graduation and had spotted her a couple of times at his parties. Even from a distance the woman looked anything but ordinary.

Blonde and still beautiful, Mrs Garrison oozed the sort of sleek glamour only bags of money could bring. Michele had no doubt her working-class ways had long gone the way of her working-class background, replaced by the panache and ultra-sophisticated style which distinguished Sydney's social set from the ordinary.

'That may well be,' Michele argued. 'But I still don't fancy spending another month's salary on another dress which I'll only wear once. Unlike some people, I don't live rent-free. I have a mortgage to pay!'

Tyler's sucked-in breath made her feel a bit guilty. Was she being petty? Maybe, but too bad! If he couldn't stand the heat then he could get out of the kitchen. Which translated to...if he didn't like what she dished out, then he could dump her right then and there!

Michele ignored the niggling thought that she was being deliberately obnoxious to make him dump her, thereby avoiding any future dilemmas, decisions or disasters.

'You're coming,' Tyler growled. 'Even if I have to buy you a bloody dress myself!'

'No, you won't,' she retorted. 'You might think you can buy whatever you want in life, Tyler Garrison, but you can't buy me!'

'I'm well aware of that,' he snapped. 'I'm not trying to buy you, woman. I'm trying to get you to come out with me Friday night. Damn it all, it's hard enough waiting till then to see you again. You don't honestly think I could stand waiting till Saturday night, do you?'

The confession took her breath away. Till she realised he was talking about sex. She supposed it wasn't often Tyler had to go a whole five days without it.

Still, his wanting her this badly sparked the wickedest response in her, even over the phone.

'You could always come over to my place tonight,' she said, her voice low and warm and sexy.

'I could. But not for long enough. I told you...I'll be working night and day all this week. Now, stop being a tease and say you'll come Friday night.'

Her laugh was knowing. 'I dare say I will.'

'Michele! I'm shocked at you!' But his voice was smiling.

'No, you're not. You're not shocked at all,' she said,

smiling too, if a little ruefully. 'You're a very corruptive force, Tyler Garrison. And you're far too used to getting your own way with women.'

'So you *will* come?'

'Would you like to rephrase that?'

'Will you accompany me to my parents' anniversary dinner party on Friday night?'

'I suppose so. What time?'

'I'll pick you up at seven.'

'And what do you think I should wear?'

'As little as possible!'

CHAPTER TEN

'ARE YOU sure you don't mind my borrowing this dress?' Michele asked as she smoothed the wine-red dress down over her hips, then twisted so that she could see the back view in Lucille's full-length mirror.

It was Monday evening, and Michele had knocked on Lucille's door after dinner to ask her where she might buy something suitable for a swanky dinner party. After further questioning, Lucille had insisted she had just the thing in her own wardrobe, and drawn Michele into her bedroom for a try-on.

The dress certainly had style, and a subtle glamour which appealed to Michele. A simple sheath face-on, with a high, wide neckline and long, tight sleeves, it had a daring back, with a deep V cut to the waist, and cross-over straps holding it together.

'What if I spill some food on it?' she asked worriedly.

'I'm sure it's dry-cleanable,' Lucille replied airily from where she was sitting on the bed, watching her friend. 'I don't wear it any more, anyway. I saw it in the window of one of those designer boutiques at their end-of-winter sale last year and couldn't resist the fifty per cent off. But after wearing it the once, and having to fend off the men all night, I decided not to give it another airing till I'd lost at least ten pounds. Which is simply not going to happen. I'm far too fond of doughnuts. You can have it, if you like.'

'Oh, no, no, no! I couldn't let you give it to me. It must have cost a bomb, even at fifty per cent off. I can tell. The material is utterly gorgeous, for starters. It doesn't crush at all, does it?' It also moulded itself to Michele's body like a second glove. She could understand why, on Lucille's more voluptuous figure, it might have caused a riot, especially since one could hardly wear a bra with that back.

'Let me pay you something for it,' Michele insisted.

'Absolutely not. It's a gift.'

Michele was quite moved. 'Are you sure?'

Lucille's lovely mouth beamed at her. 'Of course I'm sure. It made me look like a tart, whereas you look simply divine. Take it and knock the Garrison women dead in it. They wouldn't dare look down their noses at you wearing an original Orsini, I can assure you.'

'An Orsini! Oh, my God, is it really?'

'The tag's there to prove it. Wear those sexy black shoes you bought for the wedding and you'll be the belle of the ball. Well…the darling of the dinner party, anyway. Plus you'll be back in bed with the son and heir before you can say Jack Robinson. Which is the only reason you're going, I hope,' she added firmly. 'Sex is the name of the game here, Michele, and don't you forget it. Casanova's not taking you home to meet Mummy and Daddy because he's planning on proposing. The only proposals men like him make are designed to get women flat on their back and keep them there.'

Michele knew Lucille was right. But she still found her voicing the reality of their relationship out loud really depressing.

Lucille cocked her head on one side and frowned.

'What *now*?' Michele sighed.

'Earrings!' Lucille pronounced, already scrambling off the bed. 'You need long, dangling sexy earrings with that dress. I have some black crystal ones here which will be perfect, though these I *do* want back again. Oh, and you need to go back to that same hairdresser and get him to put your hair up.'

'Hair up,' Michele repeated rather wearily. 'And long, dangling sexy earrings. Where will it all end?'

Which was the question she carried with her for the rest of the week. And while she was dressing on the Friday night.

But when she looked at the finished product in the mirror, her reflection dazzled her so much that all worry was temporarily banished from her mind, replaced by the most seductive excitement.

The dress had looked good the other night. But with her hair up, full make-up on and the black crystal earrings dangling it was a triumph, transforming her into a sleek, sexy stranger who radiated a sophistication and style she hadn't known she had in her. The blue dress had been pretty, but this was something else!

Slipping on the killer black shoes, Michele walked slowly in a complete circle, marvelling at the way the dress moved on her body. Not only moved, but shimmered. She hadn't noticed the shimmer so much the other night.

Her security intercom suddenly buzzing sent her whirling round. It was only ten to seven. Tyler was early. That was...if it *was* Tyler.

All of a sudden Michele was swamped by the most awful feeling it might be Kevin, which was crazy. He was probably still on his honeymoon.

But the suspicion persisted as she walked with escalating tension towards her front door. Her hand hovered for a second before switching off the buzzer. 'Who is it?' she asked warily.

'One very impatient man,' Tyler replied, and Michele could not contain her sigh of relief. 'I've finally put that damned magazine to bed and I'm here for some rest and recreation.'

'Thank heaven for that,' she muttered as she pressed the button which released the security door before racing back into her bedroom to get her purse together in the minute it would take him to get up the stairs. She was just giving herself a liberal spray of Knowing perfume when the doorbell rang.

'Coming,' she called as she bolted back, amazed at how quickly she could move in those shoes when she wanted to.

'You're early,' she said, on sweeping open the door.

Tyler's shock was gratifying, as was the way he looked her up and down. If she hadn't been feeling excited before, she certainly was now, with this gorgeous man eating her up with his eyes.

And she meant *gorgeous*!

Tyler in a tux had been resplendent. But Tyler in a casual grey lounge suit and an open-necked blue shirt was so scrumptious it was downright unfair. How she could be expected to keep her hands off him till after a sit-down five-course meal, she had no idea!

He began shaking his head at her, his expression both amused and reproachful. 'You bad, bad girl.'

Michele's chin lifted saucily. 'What do you mean?'

'You know damned well what I mean. My tongue was already hanging out before I got here. But that's nothing to what I'm going to be feeling after looking at you in that get-up all night. I suppose you wouldn't consider a quickie before we leave, would you?'

Michele not only considered it, she was seriously tempted.

But pride rescued her. Plus her long-practised habit of never agreeing with Tyler on principle. She found she could still do that quite easily, provided she wasn't in his arms at the time.

'And have my hundred-dollar hairdo ruined?' she scoffed. 'Not to mention the dress.'

Tyler gave it another, closer inspection. 'I'll bet that set you back more than a hundred.'

'Actually, it was free. Lucille gave it to me.'

'Lucille?'

'She's a neighbour. And a good friend. They're her earrings as well, so if you think I've gone out and spent a fortune trying to impress the Garrisons, then you can think again!'

'Heaven forbid I should think such a thing,' he returned drily.

'I also don't go in for quickies.'

'In that case I suggest you bring something to put on in the morning. But don't bother with a nightie.'

She gaped at him, whereupon he gave her a droll look.

'I'm presuming you won't have any objection to staying the night at my place. I would like to have some wine at the dinner party, and I never drink and drive these days.'

'In that case hold my purse while I go throw a few things in a bag.' Michele wasn't about to put up a fight. Staying the night at Tyler's place was exactly what she wanted to do, so there was no point in coming the moral high ground at this stage. Or in trying to annoy Tyler simply for the sake of it.

Though old habits *did* die hard.

'I popped in my own toothbrush as well,' she quipped, on returning with a plastic shopping bag containing a change of clothes and a few toiletries. 'I dare say you keep a supply of such things in your bathroom for unexpected overnight guests, but I prefer to use my own.'

'Michele,' he said warningly.

'Yes, Tyler?'

'You have the wrong idea about me.'

'No, I don't, Tyler. I have exactly the right idea about you.'

'Maybe I was like that once. But not now.'

'A leopard can't change its spots.'

'It could if the spots were only painted on in the first place.'

'Huh?'

'Oh, never mind! Come along. I don't want to argue. I've been looking forward to tonight all week.'

Suddenly Michele felt guilty over trying to get a rise out of him. Maybe he couldn't change, but he hadn't been anything but honest with her. The least she could be was be honest back.

'So have I,' she admitted with a soft sigh, and his head snapped round, their eyes clashing.

As much as she doubted Tyler's ability to sustain an intimate relationship with any woman, Michele could not doubt the desire for her which was smouldering in his eyes at that moment.

'I've been wanting you,' he groaned. 'So very, very badly.'

'I felt the same way,' she confessed, perhaps stupidly. But it was true. 'I couldn't even concentrate at work.'

'This damned dinner is going to be hell.'

'It'll build our characters.'

'Our characters! There's nothing wrong with either of our characters!'

'That's a matter of opinion,' she countered. 'Think of the desserts, then. That usually puts you in a good humour.'

'The only dessert I want is one very sweet and sexy brunette.'

Michele's face flamed. 'You...you have to stop talking about things like that.'

Tyler grinned. 'Ah. Getting to you, is it?'

'I refuse to be corrupted further,' she said loftily, while her imagination raged.

'We still have at least five minutes before we have to leave,' he suggested wickedly. 'I promise I won't muss your hair or ruin your dress. You won't even have to take off your shoes.'

'Out!' she ordered. And hit him with the plastic bag. She kept on hitting him all the way down the stairs.

CHAPTER ELEVEN

THE GARRISON mansion was situated on a prime harbourside site in the exclusive eastern suburb of Point Piper. It was surrounded by a high stone security wall and eight-feet high electronically controlled gates through which Tyler drove with surprising sedateness twenty minutes later.

He didn't, however, proceed around the circular gravel driveway to the impressive steps which led up to the marble-columned portico. He directed his car towards the six-car garage at the side of the house.

Zapping open the two huge roller doors as he approached, Tyler guided his new green Honda into a spare spot to the right of a blue BMW and a red Mazda. The doors rolled down sedately behind them even before Michele had finished getting out.

'Cleo's car?' she asked, pointing to a silvery-blue Aston Martin parked two spaces away against the far wall. It had a dented mudguard and a big scratch along one door.

'Yep,' Tyler confirmed. 'I never park anywhere near it. That girl drives like a lunatic.'

'Unlike her brother, who is suddenly driving very carefully in a very conservative car. Are we perhaps down to our last points on our licence?' she teased.

'Not at all,' he replied with a perfectly straight face. 'It's the new me. The leopard without its spots.'

'Goodness. I'm impressed.'

'I should hope so.'

'So, shall I leave my things in your car or shall we take them down to your place first?' It was quite a walk down past the terraced gardens and the pool area to the converted boat-house which Tyler lived in.

His eyes flashed. 'Best leave them in the car. I don't trust myself alone with you just now.'

Michele had to laugh, despite feeling somewhat the same way. The drive over in his car had been claustrophobic, to say the least, the atmosphere thick with sexual tension.

Now, as she stood facing Tyler across the bonnet of his car, she wondered if sex was the sum total of why he was dating her, and whether all that talk about leopards changing their spots was just that.

Talk.

Tyler had always liked to banter with her, always liked to take the opposite point of view once she'd expressed an opinion. If she said something was white, he'd argue it was black. It she accused him of being shallow, he'd claim he was deep. It wasn't just her who'd been contrary over the years, especially back at uni. He'd often deliberately picked an argument with her during those four years, seemingly enjoying the hours of verbal to and fro as they'd both battled to win their points. Kevin had usually walked off and left them to it.

In hindsight, Michele realised she'd developed a

love/hate relationship with those arguments. They'd been stimulating intellectually whilst at the same time definitely irritating. Many was the time she'd wanted to turn the verbal into the physical, as she had back at her place with that plastic bag. The urge to hit him sometimes had been acute, spurring her on to even more verbal assaults.

Now she wondered if she'd just wanted an excuse to touch him. Any excuse.

Was that why she'd agreed to become Tyler's next girlfriend? To finally satisfy a lust which had simmered in a semi-dormant and highly unsatisfactory state for a decade...?

'Tyler,' she said, still puzzling over her thoughts.

His handsome face registered instant wariness. 'Oh-oh. Somehow I don't like the sound of that "Tyler".'

'I was just thinking...'

'Even worse,' he groaned.

'Don't be silly. There's no point in us pretending any more, is there? I mean...we're not still at Kevin's wedding.'

Michele wasn't prepared for the wintry anger which swept into his eyes, turning them cold, bleak blue. 'I thought I'd made it quite clear that I'm not pretending anything with you any more. God, Michele, I—'

'No, no,' she broke in as she tossed everything she was holding onto the passenger seat, then banged the car door shut. 'You've got me wrong. That's not what I meant.' She made her way round to where Tyler was still standing by his door, looking totally gorgeous and totally exasperated with her.

'Look,' she started again, choosing her words more carefully. 'For all our faults and flaws, we've always been honest with each other. I mean, you've called me a silly fool to my face and I've called you... Oh, goodness knows how many things. And we were both probably right about each other. But did it ever occur to you that some of my too brutal candour might have been sparked by something other than honesty? You said you'd wanted to sleep with me for ages. It just came to me that maybe I've been the same way. Maybe it even goes right back to our first days at uni. Maybe what I wanted back then was not to make war with you so much as make love?'

She'd stunned him. She could see it in his eyes. And in his body language. His nostrils flared as he sucked in a startled breath. His back stiffened and straightened, as did his shoulders.

Immediately Michele realised her mistake. It had still come out sounding all wrong, as though she'd been suffering from some long-unrequited love for him. Hardly the sort of thing a man like Tyler liked to hear from *any* girl, let alone one he'd always called far too sentimental and sensitive; one who always wore her heart on her sleeve and clung to a man even when he didn't want to be clung to any more.

He was probably expecting her to declare her undying love any minute and was horrified at the prospect.

Panic that she would be dumped before this night was out spurred her into instant damage limitation mode. She reached up to make soothing strokes down his jacket lapels whilst she smiled up at him.

'Silly me,' she said. 'I didn't mean *make love* so much as *have sex*. How could I really make love with you when I was in love with Kevin? But you know what I mean, Tyler. Sex is another thing entirely to love, even for women, I've found, since last weekend.'

She stopped stroking his lapels when he grabbed her hands and threw them back by her sides.

'Well, it *is*!' she insisted. 'No need to look so disgusted. We females have our carnal sides too, you know, not always connected with our consciences or common sense. I'm sure it's perfectly viable for a woman to love one man whilst still wanting another. And let's face it, Tyler, you *are* one gorgeous man. Underneath my surface hostility, I always did think so.'

Once Tyler's anger was safely on the wane Michele warmed to the task of finding out an answer to the question which had been plaguing her all week.

'I realise now I wouldn't have been a normal heterosexual female if I hadn't secretly fancied you all along. Of course, that doesn't explain why you might have fancied me in return, given your penchant for girls who rate a perfect ten in looks. So what was the attraction for you? Forbidden fruit, perhaps, because I was Kevin's girlfriend? Or just a challenge because I didn't instantly fall to my knees in adoration before you at first sight? Kevin seemed to think your male ego had to be involved, since I'm no stunner.'

She hadn't meant to bring up Kevin. She'd simply

wanted the truth. But, as usual with Tyler, she'd put her foot in her mouth. What was it she wanted him to say, for pity's sake?

Shame was already forming an apology on her lips when Tyler's hands shot out to grab her by the shoulders. He yanked her hard against him, but didn't kiss her as she'd thought he was going to. He simply smiled down into her startled face with a chilling little smile which sent a shiver ripping down her spine.

'You think you know me, don't you?' he said with soft menace. 'You have no idea. No idea at all. As for Kevin's opinion...spare me his insights into my character and motives, thank you very much. Although, yes, I admit my ego does come into play here. As does your own. Oh, yes, you've got quite a big ego, honey. You don't like to lose. At anything. That's why you kept taking Kevin back.'

Michele knew what he was saying held some truth in it. But she resented his saying so. Very much.

'So what do you want to hear, Michele?' he taunted back. 'That I fell in love with you at first sight? That I've been craving your company, both in bed and out, for a decade? That I've accepted the crumbs you've thrown me—and the insults—because I was besotted and obsessed with you?'

His mockery hurt far more than his fingertips digging into her shoulders. 'That's hardly a proper answer,' she threw at him, no longer ashamed. Just angry.

'There is no proper answer, honey,' he growled. 'Only an improper one. The basic fact is I wanted to get into your pants the first day I saw you. Yes, it annoyed the hell out of me that you took absolutely no notice of me. And, yes, it made me want to spew whenever I saw you being all lovey-dovey with Kevin. And, yes, it infuriated me every time you went back to him!'

'Then why didn't you make a move on me any of those numerous times Kevin and I split up?' she challenged.

'Because I knew you hadn't finished with him and I don't believe in setting myself up to be dumped.'

'You didn't want to get into my pants all that much, then, did you? I've seen you in action when you go into seduction mode, and, brother, you're a hard act to resist.'

'How flattering of you to say so. I'm forced to admit, however, that by then having sex with you wasn't the highest priority in my life.'

'Oohh...' Her face burned with a shaming mixture of hurt and humiliation as she wrenched out of his grasp. 'You bastard.' When she lifted her hand to hit him, he snatched it, then grabbed her other rapidly rising hand.

'But that was before last weekend,' he muttered as he backed her up against the car door, effectively imprisoning her against him. '*Now*, having sex with you is in danger of becoming more than my highest priority,' he grated out, grinding himself against her. 'I suspect it's about to become a necessity. I'm going to need it like I need food, or water, or air. To live. God, Michele...'

His kiss was beyond hunger, beyond anything Michele had ever experienced before. Incredibly arousing in more than the physical, because it also exploited her weakness for being needed.

And whilst Tyler's need was only sexual, it was more powerful than anything she'd ever known with Kevin. It called to the primal woman in her, demanding she surrender to Tyler's male dominance.

Her back automatically arched as she pressed her breasts harder against his chest, her head tipping backwards in an attitude of erotic submission. He groaned, then muttered something unintelligible against her bruised lips as he tore his away.

She moaned in protest. But he wasn't abandoning her. His mouth merely had another objective, swooping to the base of her exposed throat, brushing one of the black crystal earrings on the way, setting it swinging wildly against her suddenly goose-bumped skin. He ignored her startled cry and clamped his lips into her flesh.

Michele groaned when he started to suck, her head clunking right back onto the bonnet of the car. When Tyler abruptly let her hands go she had to press her palms against the car, lest she sink to the garage floor on her jelly-like knees. His now free hands fell to her hips, where he started dragging her skirt upwards, past her knees, her thighs. She knew what he was going to do but she didn't care. She didn't care about anything but giving him what he wanted. And what *she* now wanted.

The sound of a door being opened into the garages

preceded the most appalling silence. Tyler's hands and mouth had stopped at the sound. So had Michele's heart. If her eyes hadn't already been shut, she would have shut them.

So it was perverse that they defied her to flutter open.

Cleo was standing in the open doorway, her eyes a wintry blue as they surveyed the scene before her. She looked coolly elegant in a pale blue silk pants suit and cream camisole, pearls at her throat and in her ears. Her blonde hair was up, not softly, like Michele's, but swept back severely in a style that would have been hard on anyone with less than perfect features.

Finally she spoke, in the coldest and most caustic of voices. 'I do so hate to interrupt, brother dear, but Mummy was wondering what was keeping you. Shall I tell her you'll only be a little while longer?'

Michele wanted to just die. Embarrassment crawled like spiders all over her.

Tyler gave a small shudder before smoothing Michele's skirt back down, then levering her upright from the car.

'Don't be such a supercilious hypocrite, Cleo,' he grated out as he turned to face his sister. 'I've found you in worse predicaments. So I got a bit carried away for a while there. I haven't seen Michele all week, so it's only natural. Sorry, darling,' he directed at a still shaky Michele, smiling warmly as he wound a loving arm around her waist. 'You can smack my hand later. Right, Cleo. Off you go. We're right behind you.'

'Michele can't possibly go in to meet our parents

looking like that,' Cleo snapped, before Tyler had taken a single step.

'Looking like what? She looks gorgeous.'

'She has a love bite on her neck the size of Texas!'

Michele's hand flew up to cover the offending spot whilst her face flamed.

Tyler lifted her trembling hand and peered closely. 'Mmm. Got any make-up with you?' he asked softly.

'O…only lipstick. And it's in the car.'

Tyler looked at her lips. 'I don't think you need lipstick. Your lips are pink enough. I'm so sorry,' he whispered, his eyes apologising profusely.

'Oh, for pity's sake, I have some pancake make-up in my room which should do the trick,' Cleo offered impatiently. 'Michele, you come with me. Tyler, stop that lovey-dovey nonsense and get yourself along to the front living room. Poor Hugh is getting the third degree from Dad, and Mummy's beginning to look tense. Unfortunately Aunt Ivy and Uncle John couldn't make it, so there's just the six of us.'

'Best do what she says,' Tyler muttered in Michele's ear. 'Your throat does look like you've had a run-in with Dracula.'

Michele didn't wonder. Though still embarrassed, she wasn't angry with him. How could she be when he was being so sweet? Besides, she'd been as much to blame. 'Are you sure you don't have a coffin hidden down under the boat-house?' she murmured.

Tyler laughed. 'You've discovered my secret. Now, off you go with Cleo while I go rescue poor Hugh.'

'Who's poor Hugh?' Michele asked as she trailed

after Tyler's sister into the house and up some narrow back stairs.

'He's the man I was thinking of marrying. But I'm not so sure after the pathetic display he's given this evening so far,' she added waspishly. 'There's nothing turns me off quicker than when my boyfriends don't stand up to my father. Here we are…' They'd reached an upper hallway by then, and Cleo threw open a door on her right, ushering Michele inside.

It was nothing like Michele would have imagined Cleo's bedroom to be, other than huge. Her guess would have been a decor in cool colours, with a modern, classy look, like its occupant.

Instead it was sweetly feminine, in pink and white, with frills and flounces. The bed was a four-poster, painted white, with a pink lace quilt and squillions of white lace cushions resting on it, threaded with pink ribbon. Silver-framed photographs covered the walls on either side of the bed, depicting Cleo from babyhood upwards.

'I know,' Cleo said drily, on seeing Michele's surprised expression. 'It's awful, isn't it? Mummy had it decorated for me like this for my tenth birthday and I hated it even then. But I didn't have the heart to tell her. She said it was the bedroom she always wanted as a little girl, but never had. So I hugged her and said I loved it to death. Now I wouldn't change it for the world. It plays tapes in my head of my childhood, which was so blissfully happy, of a world before the problems of adulthood warp one's views of everything.'

Michele was amazed, both by the sentiments expressed and the wistful softness which crept into Cleo's eyes when she spoke of her mother and her childhood. Who would have believed that underneath the cold snobbishness lay a deep-feeling and sensitive soul?

Suddenly becoming aware that she was being stared at, Cleo let her face harden once more. 'Now that I have you alone, there's something I want to say to you.'

'Oh? What?' Michele stiffened inside, knowing this wasn't going to be pleasant.

'Tyler has told me in no uncertain terms that I'm to butt out where you and he are concerned, but I wanted to warn you that if you hurt my brother then I'll—'

'Hurt *Tyler*?' Michele broke in, astonished by the warning, and more than a little angry. 'How could I possibly hurt Tyler? I think the boot's on the other foot, don't you? Tyler's the one with the fast reputation around here, not me. It'll be Tyler who ends this relationship first, not the other way around.'

'I doubt that very much,' Cleo said coldly.

'And what does that mean?'

'Nothing,' Cleo muttered, whirling away and stalking over to her dressing table, where she started rummaging around in a drawer. 'I've said too much already.'

'Too damned right you have. What your brother and I do together *is* none of your business, as he so rightly pointed out. But since rudeness is the order of the day, then I've got a question for you. Just what is it about me that you don't like? Because you've never liked me. You didn't like me even when I was Kevin's girl-friend.'

Cleo spun round, a panstick of foundation in her hand. 'You really want to know?'

'Yes, I really want to know.'

'Well, for starters it used to bug me that you never bothered to dress properly when you came to any of Tyler's parties, not even the more formal ones here in the house. You'd just show up in any old thing. You never made any effort at all. But I see that's all changed now. I recognise an Orsini when I see one. Not to mention the suddenly glamorous hair and make-up. Which means your agenda's changed, hasn't it?'

'My...agenda?'

'Oh, don't come that innocent act with me. You're a smart girl. You know what I'm talking about. You've decided to set your cap at Tyler. I just haven't worked out yet if you're planning to marry my brother out of cold-blooded ambition, or some kind of sick revenge after your beloved Kevin dumped you for Danni.'

Michele's mouth fell open with shock before snapping shut again. 'My God, where on earth do you get off, insulting me like that? I'll have you know that if and when I get married it will because I'm in love with my husband-to-be, not for money, and certainly not for revenge. Maybe girls like you marry for reasons other then true love, but not me! Look, forget the make-up. I'm out of here!'

Panic banished all enmity from Cleo's face in a flash. 'No, no, you can't go! Tyler will kill me!'

'Then you have a big problem, because if I don't go, then *I'll* kill you. So if you want me to stay then I suggest you apologise profusely and promise to be very, very polite for the rest of the night.'

Cleo's blue eyes blazed before she grudgingly accepted defeat. 'You're right,' she muttered. 'I'm sorry. I was way out of line. It's just that...'

'That what?'

'Nothing,' she muttered. 'Let's get that neck of yours fixed up.'

Michele stood tautly still while Cleo tried to cover up the bruise with some pancake foundation. 'Whatever possessed Tyler to give you a love bite just before he brought you in to meet Mum and Dad?' Cleo muttered irritably as she dabbed.

'I don't think love had much to do with it,' Michele said wryly. 'Which is why you're worrying about me for nothing. I honestly thought you'd know your brother better than this. No matter what you think of me and my motives, marriage isn't on *Tyler's* agenda. All Tyler wants from me, Cleo, is what you saw in the garage. As I said before, if anyone gets hurt in this affair it will be me, not Tyler.'

Cleo lifted her head to frown at Michele. 'Are you saying you really care about him?'

'More than I should. But don't tell him that.'

'Why not?' she asked, and Michele laughed.

'Because my loving him is the last thing Tyler

wants. Goodness, Cleo, you really don't know your brother very well, do you? Come on, that will have to do. If we don't go downstairs soon, Tyler will come looking for us, and I don't think you'd want that, would you?'

CHAPTER TWELVE

CLEO LED Michele back downstairs via the more impressive front staircase, then on into the formal lounge room which Michele had never seen before. It had always been off-limits to Tyler's parties.

As she walked in and glanced around, she could understand why. It was full of richly covered sofas and chairs, along with the most exquisitely carved coffee and side tables on which perched delicate sculptures and porcelain figurines. Not the sort of room you'd want boisterous partygoers racing around, knocking into things and spilling drinks. The plush cream carpet alone would not have survived such treatment.

A huge fireplace dominated the wall opposite the double door entry, swiftly drawing Michele's eyes. Tyler and the same dark-haired yuppie who'd accompanied Cleo to the wedding were propping up opposite ends of the marble mantelpiece, under which a fire was softly glowing.

'Poor Hugh' looked somewhat nervous as he twirled his drink agitatedly in his hands. Tyler was more relaxed, sipping straight Scotch on the rocks. Mr Garrison was standing at a large drinks cabinet in one corner, mixing something equally potent. His wife was elegantly settled at one end of the gold brocade sofa, a martini at her lips.

Michele couldn't name a designer label on first sight, but she knew that the black gown draped superbly around the woman's still great figure would have cost the earth. And if she wasn't mistaken those were real diamonds dripping from Mrs Garrison's throat and ears.

Tyler's eyes bored like laser beams into his sister when they entered, before softening on Michele. His warm smile sent her stomach curling over and the most appalling realisation blasting into her brain. She didn't just care about Cleo's playboy brother. She'd done what Lucille had warned her against. She'd fallen in love with him!

Dismay had no time to set in before Mrs Garrison spotted her.

'So there you are at long last!' she exclaimed in a nicely normal voice, nothing at all like Cleo's exclusive girls' school accent. 'Come over here, Michele, and sit by me. I want to find out how it is that I've never spoken to you before when Tyler tells me you've been coming here to his parties for years.' She patted the cushion next to her and smiled at Michele, who found herself warming to the woman, despite having expected just the opposite.

'I'm just going to check to see if the caterers need anything,' Cleo said, leaving Michele to walk alone across the room and sit down next to her mother. She managed without tripping, a mean feat in such thick carpet and in those shoes.

'You know, dear, I have to confess I don't even recognise you,' Tyler's mother said with sweet sheepishness. 'Which is simply terrible. Though I do have a terrible memory for faces and names, don't I, Tyler? Get Michele a drink will you, love? You must know what she likes.'

'Champagne always goes down well, I've found,' he said with a rakish gleam in his eyes, levering himself away from the mantelpiece and striding over to join his father.

Michele watched him with new lovestruck eyes, and wondered how he had captivated her heart without her knowing. Desire for him she could well understand, but where had the love come from? She'd thought she had to still be in love with Kevin after all the years they'd spent together. She'd thought she was safe from this type of dilemma…at least for a while.

Anger joined her dismay. How dared Tyler make her love him when he didn't want her love? And when she didn't, either. She'd wanted to have fun for a while, as he'd promised her, without any thought of the past, or the future, or anything. She'd wanted to just float, emotionally, whilst her battered heart mended, enjoying nothing but the moment and, yes, the sex.

And now…now she had to contend with the ultimate pain of another failure in her personal life, another poor decision, another looming disaster.

What was it Lucille had said to her the other day? Something about Tyler being a pretty unforgettable person…

Michele's eyes drifted back to Tyler, her beautiful

but fickle Tyler, and her heart almost broke then and there.

'Tyler tells us you're in advertising,' his mother was saying. 'Quite a high-up position, too. You must be very clever.'

'More than clever, Mum,' Tyler joined in as he brought Michele her glass of champagne. 'She even beat me at *Quick off the Mark* the other night.'

'And why not?' his mother said. 'You don't know everything, even if you think you do.'

Tyler laughed. 'Don't worry. She won't beat me next time. I've been practising.' And he winked at her.

The thought of playing more games of any kind with Tyler brought Michele such pain that she almost groaned aloud. Every survival instinct she had told her to cut and run, but love had always made her weak.

So she stayed and she smiled. She smiled so much her mouth ached.

Perversely, she found out over the next few hours that both Tyler's parents were the nicest people, and the best parents. They really talked to both Tyler and Cleo, treating them as adults yet never forgetting they were their children, to be loved and cared about. That was why poor Hugh got the third degree. Because he had to pass muster if he wanted to marry Cleo. Michele could well understand that. Fortunately Hugh found his feet some time during the main course, and spoke up for himself quite well.

Cleo began to look happy for the first time that night.

It crossed Michele's mind that her own father

wouldn't give a damn whom she married, as long as she never came home to live again. He'd not hidden his relief when she'd moved out as soon as she'd finished uni and was earning her own money.

Tyler's father, however, sounded as if he never really wanted his children to leave home. A big, broad-shouldered man, he had piercing blue eyes and a handsome though weathered face, which bespoke too many days spent out sailing, or playing polo.

'This boy of mine has done a brilliant job with that magazine,' he told Michele proudly over dessert. 'I won't have any worries about retiring in a few years. All he needs now is the right wife and I'll be completely happy.'

Visual daggers were launched at him from several quarters, not the least of which was Tyler. He even stopped eating his second helping of mango cheesecake to look up and glare at his father.

'All right, all right, I know I shouldn't mention the dreaded M word. But I wouldn't be a normal father if I didn't want to see you settled with a family of your own. What do you think, Michele? Tyler says you've been good friends for over a decade now, so you won't mind my asking you. Don't you think it's high time he was married?'

Michele took a few moments to steady her heart. 'I think, Mr Garrison,' she said, in what she hoped was a calm, cool voice, 'that Tyler will come round to thoughts of marriage and children in his own good time. He's always known what he wants in life and has no trouble getting it. When he decides on having a family, I'm sure he'll swiftly persuade some lovely girl that being his wife and the mother of his children is what *she* wants as well.'

'Well said!' Mr Garrison pronounced. 'And you're quite right. I should have more faith in the boy.'

'"The boy",' Tyler ground out, 'is sitting right here and can speak for himself.'

'Speak, then!' his father challenged. 'Tell us your views on the subject.'

'My views on marriage are very much a reflection on why we're all here tonight.' He stood up and lifted his glass of wine. One of several he'd downed over dinner, Michele had noticed. 'Let me propose a toast which will explain my feelings on the matter. To my wonderful parents, on this, their thirty-fifth wedding anniversary. You have set a perfect example of what marriage should be. True partnership based on mutual love, mutual respect and mutual goals. Till I find all that with one woman I would not dare enter such a difficult and demanding union. It would spell disaster. But that doesn't stop me admiring a man who was lucky enough to marry his true soul-mate and who has the good sense to cherish her every day of his life! To my father, Richard, and my lovely mother, Marion!'

Michele stared up at Tyler, moved and confused by his words. How could a man express such beautiful sentiments yet live his life in such a shallow fashion? It didn't make sense.

She struggled to find an answer. Perhaps he'd simply never met a girl who'd even come close to being his soul-mate.

Not that he'd given himself much of a chance, she thought irritably. It took longer than a few weeks to get to know anyone. Knowing someone in the biblical sense wasn't at all the same.

Michele shook her head and looked away. Truly, she felt quite angry with the man. Didn't he know how lucky he was to come from such a close and loving family? He should be capable of a little more emotional depth! Dating one girl after another strictly for sexual variety was the stuff creeps were made of.

Yet Tyler was not a creep. Not at all! Maybe he'd just got into terrible habits because he was beautiful and rich and girls made it so darned easy for him to use them that way.

Like you, you mean, came the dry little reminder.

'And now I'd like to make another toast,' Tyler was saying.

Michele did her best to concentrate on the moment, and not the simply awful decision she was going to be forced to make in the morning.

'To Hugh,' he said, with a wink Cleo's way, 'who handled himself very well tonight under pressure.'

They all laughingly toasted Hugh. Then Cleo. Then the current issue of Tyler's magazine, at which point Michele realised Tyler was more than a little under the influence.

His mother must have come to the same conclusion. 'I think I'd better go get some strong coffee,' she said drily.

The dinner drew to a swift end after coffee, Tyler's parents retiring to their room and Hugh taking Cleo on to some club. Which left Michele and Tyler to collect her things from his car and make their way down to the boat-house.

The night was fresh and cool by then, the black sky full of stars. Tyler slid a warm arm around her shoulders, pulling her close and bending to gave her light kisses as they walked.

A deep dismay threatened to overwhelm Michele at his tenderness, because she knew it was motivated by lust, not love. Valiantly, she vowed not to dwell on this, or on what she'd decided to do the following day. Since tonight was going to be her last night with Tyler, she aimed to make it a night to remember. Tonight she would make love to him with her heart, as well as her body.

'So what do you think of my family now?' he asked when he stopped to unlock the boat-house door and switch on the lights.

'Your parents are wonderful.'

'And Cleo?'

'She's improving…'

'I think she's beginning to like you,' he said, and Michele gave him a sceptical look. 'No, I mean it. I can tell. I can read Cleo like a book.'

'Does it matter?' she said, unable to contain a niggling irritation at this pointless line of questioning. Once the door was flung open, she dived past him into the boat-house, where she stopped with a jolt.

'Good Lord!' she exclaimed. 'It's all different!'

That was putting it mildly. It had once been the epitome of a male den—with a jukebox, pool table and huge bar, not to mention the mandatory animal skins in front of the fireplace.

'Better?' he said.

'Much.' Now it was all country comfort, a place to live in, not just have parties in. 'When did you do all this?'

'In the New Year. Cleo helped.'

'She did a great job. I love it. What about upstairs? Is that all changed as well?'

Tyler had a loft-style bedroom which had once housed a huge decadent waterbed with a black-lacquered bedhead.

'Totally. Cleo donated all the old stuff to charity.'

'Let me see it.'

'With pleasure.'

He took her hand and led her up the wooden stair-case, where she just stood and shook her head at his new bedroom, complete with country-style wooden bed and nautical print duvet. All that remained from his old room was the view.

Admittedly, that was impossible to change, unless you covered it with curtains, which would be just criminal. The wall opposite the foot of the bed and facing the harbour was all glass, from floor to ceiling. Michele had once thought how decadent it must be, making love on Tyler's bed with anyone passing on a boat being able to stare in at them. In the daytime, anyway. Possibly not at night, with all the lights off.

Now that would be really romantic.

'Can you turn off all the lights from up here?' she asked, and he frowned.

'Yes. Why?'

'Do it.'

He did, and she sighed at the sight. This was what romantic dreams were made of. And indelible memories.

It was also the stuff disasters were made of. Tyler could change his car, and his furniture. But he could not change the man inside. He was what he was, and it was futile to hope for more.

But don't think about that right now, Michele, she told herself. Just do what you want to do. Have your night to remember. The morning will come quickly enough...

With her heart thudding, she walked up to him and slowly peeled his jacket back off his shoulders, tossing it onto a nearby armchair.

When he opened his mouth to speak, she pressed her fingers against his lips. 'Hush up. I've been wanting to do this all night,' she murmured. 'And I simply can't wait any longer...'

CHAPTER THIRTEEN

MICHELE WOKE with the instant awareness that Tyler was not in the bed with her. She was snuggled down under a quilt, which she must have pulled up around herself during the night. Or maybe Tyler had done it for her.

Her eyes darted around the room but it seemed empty. She wouldn't have seen him sitting in the winged armchair facing the glass wall if he hadn't at that moment put a coffee mug down on the armrest. Even so, only his right hand was visible from where she was lying.

A glance at the clock-radio sitting on the bedside chest revealed it was five after five. A dull pre-dawn glow was spreading over the water, gradually dispelling the darkness of night.

'Tyler?' she asked softly. 'What are you doing up at this early hour? Can't you sleep?'

'I often can't sleep.'

The bleakness in his voice startled her, then worried her.

'Is...is there something wrong?'

'Wrong?' he echoed in a flat voice. 'What could possibly be wrong?'

'I don't know. But something obviously is. Why don't you come back to bed and tell me?'

'Go back to sleep, Michele.'

'But—'

'Just go back to sleep, damn you!' he snapped.

Though stunned and hurt by this outburst, Michele naturally couldn't do what he asked. What woman in love could?

Gathering up the quilt around her, she climbed from the bed and walked over to squat by the side of the chair.

Tyler was sitting there, naked. But his naked flesh held no interest for her at that moment. All she cared about was the haunted look in his eyes and the reason behind his wretchedness. She'd never seen him like this. Except that one time in hospital.

Yet this seemed somehow worse.

'Tyler, darling,' she murmured, one hand coming to rest on his nearest knee.

He looked at it and laughed. 'Yes, Michele, darling?' Sarcasm dripped from the return endearment.

Michele's hand retreated behind the quilt as she searched his face and tried to see what was troubling him. 'What's wrong?' she persisted.

His sigh sounded weary. 'I couldn't explain it to you in a million years. Let's just say I hoped things could change. But I can see they can't. I've made my bed, so to speak, and now I have to lie in it.'

'I don't know what you mean, exactly...' But she had a pretty good idea. He was telling her he couldn't change. He was what he was. A man who loved women but didn't love them. A man who, much as he might want to please his father by going the conventional path of marriage and children, simply could not embrace a lifestyle which would ultimately bore him.

'You're upset over what your father said, aren't you?'

His eyes whipped to hers in surprise.

'You want to please him by getting married,' she elaborated. 'But you know it would be wrong for you. And you're right, Tyler. To marry without love would be very wrong.'

His eyes confirmed she'd hit the nail right on the head. 'And you, Michele? Do you think you will ever marry?'

Michele shook her head. 'No,' she said heartbrokenly. 'No, I don't think so...' Lucille had been so right. Kevin she could forget. She had, hadn't she? But Tyler? No...Tyler was unforgettable. How could any other man ever measure up after him?

Michele decided not to wait to make the break.

'I...I was going to tell you in the morning,' she said bravely. 'But I think we should go back to being just good friends.'

He glared at her. 'Why? Isn't the sex good enough?'

'You know it is. But...'

'But what?' he demanded to know.

'I guess it's just not enough.'

'And what would be enough, Michele?' he sneered. 'Being in love with your lover?'

'Something like that.'

'So where does that leave you? Embracing a celibate existence for the rest of your life?'

'Probably.'

'I find it unbelievable that the girl who made love to me in such an abandoned fashion last night would give up sex altogether. I mean, let's face it, Michele, you really get off on going down on a guy, don't you? I was quite blown away, if you'll forgive the pun. I can well understand why dear old Kev kept coming back if that was what you gave him.'

She rocked back on her heels, her eyes wide with hurt and humiliation.

His groan sounded anguished. 'Dear God, I didn't mean that. Oh, hell, don't look at me like that, Michele. I'm sorry. It's just that when it was happening I thought you might have been pretending I was Kevin and, damn it all, I wanted it all to be for me!'

'It *was* all for you,' she flung at him, tears flooding her eyes. 'Couldn't you see that, you fool? Are you blind? Or don't you recognise it when a girl's fallen in love with you any more?'

He could not have been more stunned if she'd hit him.

Having said the unforgivable, she scrambled to her feet and turned her back on him, not wanting him to see the depth of her despair. 'I'm sorry,' she muttered. 'I didn't mean to say that. Just as I didn't mean to fall in love with you. I didn't want to. It…it just happened somehow…'

When she felt his presence behind her she stiffened. When he cupped her shoulders and pulled her back against him she groaned. 'Are you sure it's love you feel for me?' he murmured, his lips brushing an earlobe.

She quivered uncontrollably. 'What else could it be?'

'What else, indeed?'

She spun round in his arms. 'Are you saying you don't believe me?'

'I'm saying you could be mistaken. People do fall in love on the rebound, but it's not a lasting kind of love. Still, I'm sure it feels real at the time. So tell me, my love, when you said you wouldn't get married, were you thinking of Kevin...or me?' His watchful eyes infuriated her. Here she was, with her heart on her sleeve whilst it broke into tiny pieces and all he cared about was his infernal male ego.

'Does it matter?' she threw at him. 'It's not as though you want to marry me.'

'Ah, but I do.'

Her mouth fell inelegantly open.

'I love you,' he said. 'And I want to marry you.'

Shock swiftly gave way to anger. 'Oh, don't be ridiculous!' she spat. 'You do not!'

'See?' he scoffed. 'It's hard to believe something which doesn't seem possible because you've known a person for a long time and you have preconceived ideas about them. The irony is, Michele, *I* believe you're still in love with Kevin, and *you* believe I'm still in love with myself. Perverse, isn't it?'

She stared at him, unsure now.

'I can see the wheels ticking over,' he said drily. 'Before you add two and two and get five again, let me make a proposal.'

'Of *marriage*?' she gasped.

'Not yet. I'm not a total fool. But I do propose we keep going out together and give each other time to discover the truth.'

'About loving each other, you mean?'

He nodded. 'Exactly. Then, when we're sure we really love each other, I'll ask you to marry me again.'

Gradually the thought that Tyler *might* actually love her sank in, bringing with it a joy so bright and breath-taking that her eyes must have glowed.

'I take it that idea finds favour?'

'Oh, yes!'

'In that case I might be able to go back to bed now, and get some sleep.'

'Oh...' How could he sleep if he really loved her? Didn't he want to show her his love?

He looked at her disappointed eyes and smiled a rueful smile. 'You do realise that I've had a very hard week?'

'Yes, yes, I know...'

'And I drank more than was good for me at dinner last night.'

'Yes, I did notice...'

'And some hussy drained me dry afterwards.'

'Oh, dear... Poor Tyler...' She dropped the quilt and closed the distance between them, winding her arms up around his neck.

His eyes carried pretend panic, but his body was giving her a devastatingly different message.

'If we eventually marry,' he muttered, 'is this what I'll have to put up with all the time?'

'Only all night every night. I will want to continue working during the day.'

'What about weekends?'

'Yes, please.'

'I'll be dead by the time I'm forty!'

'I doubt it. Only the good die young.'

Michele missed the fleeting dismay in his eyes at this last remark because she was concentrating on his mouth at the time.

And then she didn't notice anything, because she was kissing the man she loved and he was kissing her back. She certainly didn't notice anything after Tyler carried her back to bed.

CHAPTER FOURTEEN

'YOU'RE on a real high, aren't you?' Lucille said as she stirred sugar into her cappuccino. 'Not only did your dress rehearsal at work go well this morning but you've found true love at last. In a rather odd place, I must admit, but who am I to question the peculiarities of life? Just don't rush into anything. Don't sign any prenuptial agreements, and when he's unfaithful after the honeymoon's over take the bastard for squillions!'

Michele laughed. 'It's no use, Lucille. Your cynicism about men is wasted on me today. If I'd had this conversation with you on Saturday morning then you might have been able to rattle me. But not today.'

'Two measly days and you're convinced? You don't think it's a mite coincidental that Daddy Garrison—who no doubt pulls the pursestrings in the family—just happened to mention he wants his son and heir married, with more little heirs on the way, and presto...said son and heir declares his love for you, with a view to matrimony?'

'Look, I know what you're saying. That thought did occur to me, too. But it just didn't hold water for long. Why me? I simply asked myself. Why not ask some gorgeous dolly-bird, if all he wants is a trophy wife to breed from? No, Lucille, Tyler loves me. I'm not sure

163

how or when or why, but he does. I can tell. He was so sweet to me over the weekend. Even the sex is different between us now.'

'How different? Surely not better? How could it possibly be better after what you told me last Monday?'

'It's not better. Just more meaningful. More… loving.'

'Look, sweetie, I don't mean to be a wet blanket. Honest. But I don't think a man as smart as Tyler would want some glamorous dolly-bird as his wife, anyway. He'd choose someone he could live with and talk to; someone he finds intelligent and interesting and yes, attractive too. He wouldn't want an ugly wife, not with his libido.'

Lucille picked up her coffee cup but it never made it to her mouth, being lowered again as she went on with her theorising. 'I wouldn't mind betting that Mr Garrison Senior has been agitating for marriage for quite a while, and finally dutiful son and heir comes up with the perfect candidate. Who better than his old friend Michele? No unknowns there. You're everything he could possibly want.

'Firstly, you've never been impressed with his money. That's good. No man likes to be the object of materialistic greed. Secondly, you're well matched, brainwise. And, finally, you were free, now that Kevin was marrying someone else. So he moves in for the kill right when he knows it will be most effective. Makes love to you like a dream after the wedding, then backs off for a whole week. Good move, that.

Then, whammo, he takes you home to Mummy and Daddy, shows himself up to be really a good guy underneath the Casanova image, and you fall for it all, hook, line and sinker!'

Michele resisted Lucille's ruthless image of Tyler all through lunch, arguing his case with all the zeal and skill of a Queen's counsel. Tyler was not and never had been a liar, she assured Lucille. He also hated users and con-men. He was not capable of a callous seduction. It did not fit his character at all!

She'd actually convinced Lucille by the time their lunch together was over. Lucille even promised to be one of the bridesmaids at their wedding. But as Michele walked slowly back to the office she realised the gloss had been taken off her happiness. Down deep, some doubts had entered her heart. When Tyler rang her within five minutes of her returning to her desk, she knew she sounded flat.

'Didn't the dress rehearsal go well?' he asked.

'Oh, yes. Quite well.'

'You sound a bit down.'

She made an effort to brighten up. 'Sorry. It's probably just a natural feeling of anticlimax after the adrenalin rush of this morning. I do get all hyped up for a presentation. It's a lot of pressure.'

'I can imagine. But from what you told me about your ideas yesterday I knew you had nothing to worry about. They're brilliant. And so are you. Changing the product name from Single-Serve Meals to Single Only Serve, then basing the whole advertising campaign on the SOS gimmick was a stroke of genius. I loved your ideas for the television commercials, especially the one on the desert island when the survivors of a shipwreck draw SOS in the sand and helicopter drops cartons of SOS meals down to them instead of rescuing them. Humour will sell something almost as well as sex.'

Michele wished he hadn't said that. But having it said did beg the question of whether that was what he'd been doing all along. Selling himself with sex.

'Michele? Are you still there?'

'Yes. Sorry. I was just thinking about the campaign. You...er...won't mention my ideas to anyone, will you? I mean...we have to play a tight hand till this Friday. Can't have the opposition knowing anything in advance.'

'My lips are sealed. Who is the opposition, do you know?'

'No. Packard Foods is being close-mouthed as well. But whoever they are, they're going in first. We're on after morning tea. They said they'd tell Harry their decision that afternoon.'

'With you at the helm, you're odds on to win.'

Michele stiffened. 'You don't have to flatter me, Tyler,' she said sharply.

His silence made her feel guilty. But compliments were a sore point with her after Kevin.

'Where do you have to go for the presentation?' Tyler went on eventually, his voice calm.

The Tyler she used to know would have snapped back at her. 'Into their head office in the city. Why?'

'Friday is Cleo's birthday. I was going to take her

for lunch somewhere. I wondered if you'd like to come too. I could book a restaurant in the city. I want you two to be friends.'

Michele didn't think she and Cleo would ever be friends. 'I don't think I should make any arrangements for Friday lunchtime, Tyler. These things sometimes run over time.'

'Very well. Now, about tonight…'

'You want to see me tonight?' Did he think he had to make love to her every night now?

'Yes. Why not? I'm not that busy this week.'

'Lucky you.'

'You really are in a mood, aren't you? I wanted to take you out to dinner and dancing. Somewhere special. You haven't let me do that yet.'

Amongst the few things she hadn't, she thought bitterly.

'I don't like to eat out on week nights.'

'Very well, I'll come over and we can eat in. You might like to show me your culinary skills.'

'I wouldn't want to overwhelm you too much with my wifely talents.'

'Are you spoiling for a fight, Michele?' he finally snapped. 'Because if you are then be careful, or you might get what you're asking for.' And he hung up.

She stared into the dead receiver, shame consuming her. What was the matter with her? How could she let Lucille taint her view of Tyler and ruin what was the best thing which had ever happened to her?

With shaking fingers she rang him straight back on his mobile. For a few frightening seconds she thought he wasn't going to answer. When he did, his voice was clipped and cold.

'Tyler, it's me,' she blurted out straight away. 'I'm so sorry. I don't know what got into me just then. I was horrid. Please forgive me. I want you to take me to dinner and dancing tonight. I really do. Please, please don't hang up on me again.'

He hesitated, and her heart stopped.

'Very well,' he said somewhat coldly. 'When?'

'When what?'

'When do you want me to pick you up tonight?'

'Oh.' She sighed her relief. 'Seven o'clock too early?'

'You'll miss *Quick off the Mark*,' he said drily.

'Stuff *Quick off the Mark*!' she exclaimed, and he laughed. It was a much happier sound.

'No, that would never do. I'll be there at seven and we'll watch it together, then leave at seven-thirty. But be warned. It's take no prisoners from now on.'

'Huh! You're dead meat, buster!'

'Dem's fightin' words, honey.'

'Put your money where your mouth is.'

'Betting money doesn't turn me on. Make it worth my while.'

'You name the stakes, then.'

'The loser gets to be the other's love slave for the night. She or he must do the other's bidding, without hesitation or equivocation.'

A frisson of excitement rippled down her spine. He really was a wicked devil. But she couldn't lose, could she? Either way, pleasure was assured. The idea, however, of his being her love slave for the night was mind-bending.

'Done!' she agreed, a little smugly. She hadn't been one hundred per cent on the ball the other time they'd played and she'd still won. This time she'd slaughter him.

'You devious devil!' she exclaimed heatedly at seven-twenty-three that night. The question part of the show had just ended, with Michele the loser by the proverbial mile. 'You deliberately let me win that other time!'

He smiled an *all the better to eat you with, my dear* smile from his chair. 'Now why would I do that?'

'Because you're a devious devil, like I just said!'

'Come now, don't be a sore loser.' He rose, looking casually glamorous in a classic blue blazer, dazzling white shirt and charcoal-grey trousers. Doing up the single button of the blazer, he strolled nonchalantly over towards the front door, where he turned slowly and smiled back at her. 'Come here, love slave.' He beckoned her over to him.

She stood up grudgingly, still smarting from her loss. But as she walked stiffly over to him the look in his eyes replaced any chagrin with wonder. Had Kevin ever looked at her like that?

She couldn't recall the occasion.

Yet she wasn't all that dolled up this time, wearing a simple enough black crêpe dress which had a matching thigh-length jacket. Her hair was down in her usual shoulder-length bob and she wasn't wearing any jewellery.

She *had* gone to some trouble with her make-up, however, highlighting her brown eyes and glossing her lips in a kiss-proof scarlet. And she'd given her perfume bottle a nudge.

Tyler seemed to like the finished package.

'What?' she asked huskily as she drew to a halt before him.

'Tell me you love me.'

She was taken aback. 'That's it? That's all you want me to do?'

His eyebrows arched coolly. 'Is it beyond you?'

'No.'

'Then say it.'

'I...I love you.'

'Not very convincing. Say it again. And add my name as well. Say, Tyler...I love you.'

'Tyler,' she said, her voice sounding thick, even to her own ears, 'I love you.'

'Much better. Now kiss me.'

'Kiss you...'

'Having trouble with your hearing tonight?'

She kissed him. A long, lingering, loving kiss of mostly lips and only a little tongue.

'Not bad,' he pronounced afterwards. 'Now, listen up, love slave. You're to tell me you love me every half-hour on the half-hour till we get back here, each time followed by a kiss. A real kiss. No matter where we are or what we're doing at the time. You are to make sure that, come the half-hour, you are not off in the Ladies' somewhere, or otherwise occupied. Do I make myself clear?'

'Yes,' she murmured, her head whirling.

It was the most romantic, and the most arousing dinner date of Michele's life. She kissed him at a set of lights on the way to a beachside restaurant, and once again at the cocktail bar. She kissed him during the entrée, twice during the main course, followed by once out on the intimate little dance floor. She kissed him again over dessert, and finally between cups of coffee, each time preceded by her declaration of love.

Every time she started to say the words he looked deep into her eyes, and she found herself telling him with just a little more passion. Her kisses got longer and hungrier. In the end she didn't care who saw her or what they thought. All she cared about was Tyler. By the time they made it back to her place she was beside herself with need for him. They didn't make it to the bedroom. Tyler took her on the floor, in the hallway, their mutual cries echoing through the darkened flat.

Michele woke the next morning feeling wonderful.

'I'm sorry about the lunch with Cleo on Friday,' she said as she snuggled up to Tyler. She'd decided she would make friends with his sister if it killed her. 'What about dinner that night instead?'

'Can't. She's going out with Hugh. Don't worry. We'll make it some other time. We have all the time in the world.'

'Yes, yes, we do, don't we?' And she smiled up at him.

He dropped a kiss on her nose. 'You were such a cute love slave.'

'And you were such a sweet master.'

'I'd rather be a sweet husband.'

Why did she flinch, then pull away from him? Surely she couldn't still doubt his intentions. He could have asked her to do anything last night, yet he'd opted for romantic requests, not raw sex.

'Still too soon for you?' Tyler said as she rose from the bed and slipped into her robe. He sounded cool about it but she could hear the underlying edge in his voice.

'A little,' she said, turning to face him.

'I see…'

She doubted he did. But it didn't seem the best time to try to explain. His face had a closed expression on it and his eyes…well, his eyes were not happy.

'How long before you might say yes to that question?' he asked rather curtly.

'Tyler, please…'

He glared at her. 'You never did know your own mind where men were concerned,' he grated out.

'That's a nasty thing to say.'

'It's the truth.' He climbed out of bed and went in search of his clothes. It took him some time. They hadn't reached the bedroom for quite a while the previous night. 'Perhaps we'd best not see each other for the rest of the week,' he pronounced harshly on his return. 'Give you time to sort out your true feelings.'

'If that's what you want,' she countered, her own chin lifting.

'I'll ring you Friday afternoon.'

'If you still want to.'

'I'll ring,' he ground out. 'You're the one dithering around here. Not me!'

She dithered for the rest of the week, sometimes filled with rage, sometimes despair, sometimes total confusion. She avoided Lucille, lest she colour her views further, and tried very hard to be fair in her judgement of Tyler. Because it wasn't her own feelings she had to sort out. It was his.

By Friday morning she'd accepted she simply wasn't convinced of his so-called love, or his motives for wanting to marry her. It was too big a change for her to swallow. From Casanova to caring conservative in one fell swoop. It just didn't ring true, no matter how she looked at it.

Harry didn't accompany his team into the city for the presentation, which Michele appreciated. She didn't need any added pressure that morning.

Packard Foods' head office was high in an office block down towards the quay, with reception rooms to rival any she'd ever seen, dauntingly spacious and extravagantly plush.

'At least it looks like they can afford us,' she muttered to her two male offsiders as they settled down to wait their turn.

Despite every confidence in the package she was about to present, swarms of butterflies still gathered in Michele's stomach. They'd arrived at ten, not wanting to be late. By ten-thirty she was a basket case. By ten-forty-five she was looking to dash to the Ladies' to throw up.

At ten-fifty-three the door to the boardroom finally opened and the opposition emerged.

Michele tried not to gape.

Kevin wasn't heading the opposition, but he was one of their huge support cast.

That Kevin's company might be their competition had never occurred to her. Given Wild Ideas was one of the two final players, she'd assumed the other candidate would be one of the smaller, boutique-style advertising agencies, not Kevin's ruthlessly go-getting international firm.

Kevin started with shock when he saw her, followed by a wry smile.

'Hello, Michele,' he said with his usual charm and gall. 'I should have known the competition might be you. Good luck. Not that you've ever needed luck.'

She totally ignored him.

Perversely, his unexpected appearance banished her nerves and brought an inner rage which focused all her energy on beating him, and his big bully of a firm.

She was brilliant, even if she had to admit it herself. When she saw the Packard people smiling and even laughing at her ad ideas, she knew Wild Ideas had the contract in the bag.

Harry was waiting at the door when they came out, a satisfied smile on his handsome face. 'You don't have to say a word,' he said. 'I heard the laughter. We're home and hosed. You can all expect a big bonus in your pay this month.'

'Thanks, Harry,' the three of them chorused.

'And take the afternoon off,' he offered magnanimously.

They exchanged shocked glances. Harry giving the afternoon off was as rare as a politician keeping his election promises.

The other two were all for a celebratory drinking session in a local bar, but Michele declined.

'Sorry, chaps,' she said in the lift on the way down to the street. 'I'm meeting someone for lunch. See you Monday.'

It was a lie, of course. She wasn't meeting anyone. Tyler was off God knew where, taking Cleo to lunch. Michele just needed to be by herself. To think, not drink. Now that the distraction of the morning was over, her personal problems pressed back in on her.

What on earth was she going to do about Tyler's proposal of marriage? She loved the man, but *marriage*? How could you knowingly go into marriage when you weren't sure of your husband-to-be's feelings for you? She couldn't bear it if he didn't really love her, or if he was unfaithful to her. And if he ever left her she would just die!

Michele strolled past Circular Quay and down to the waterfront near the Rocks. The weather was perfect. Warm, but not too warm, with only the slightest sea breeze. She was sitting at one of the open-air café tables, having a coffee by herself, when the chair next to her was wrenched out.

'Hey!' she protested, shading her eyes from the sunshine as she looked up to see the one man she didn't want to see any more that day.

'Don't you dare sit down here!' she snapped at Kevin. 'Did you follow me, damn you? I do not want to talk to you. And my anger doesn't mean I still love you,' she added scathingly. 'Far from it.'

'I know that,' he said, sitting down anyway. 'You don't honestly think I ever believed I could compete with Tyler, do you? That was just my male ego talking. Plus a healthy dose of jealousy.'

'Jealousy, my foot! Only men who care get jealous.'

'I was always jealous when you and Tyler got together. That's why I used to walk away. I don't think you realised it then, but you were probably always attracted to him. Better matched, too. Heck, kiddo, you're too smart for me.'

'Don't talk rubbish.'

'It's the truth. I was always in two minds about you. One part of me wanted to just be around you. But at the same time I hated the way you could make me feel sometimes. With you, I always had to strive to be better. I was always trying to be something I wasn't. In the end I couldn't play that game any more.'

He grimaced as though the memory actually caused him pain. But then his face softened. 'Now, with Danni, I have the upper hand both intellectually and sexually. Underneath the gloss she's a simple girl. And she adores me. It's done wonders for my self-esteem. I know you probably don't think so, but I do love her. She's a darling.'

Surprisingly, Michele felt some relief to hear this.

She didn't really wish him—or Danni—any harm. Life was too short to spend it with vengeful feelings. All she wanted now was to be happy herself.

'So are you and Tyler still dating each other?' he asked.

Michele winced at the underlying implication that it had been a whole two weeks since the wedding—an eternity in Tyler's merry-go-round love life. Pride demanded she not let Kevin see her own doubts and fears. 'Yes. And he's asked me to marry him.'

His jaw dropped. 'You're joking!'

'And why would I be joking?' she challenged.

'My God, Michele, you know what he's like. He's a great bloke, but sexual fidelity is not in his nature. He can't go a month without a new face on the pillow next to him in the morning!'

Michele wanted to defend Tyler, but suddenly she couldn't. Kevin wasn't Lucille. He knew Tyler. Maybe even better than *she* did. Guys talked to each other about sex and their various conquests. He would know exactly what made Tyler tick in that regard.

She made a choking sound as tears gushed into her eyes.

'Oh, God, Michele, don't cry,' Kevin groaned. 'Oh, hell, you're in love with him, aren't you? I mean really in love with him. Maybe more than you ever were with me.'

'Yes,' she choked out. 'I'm crazy about him.' And she snatched up a paper serviette to press against her face.

'The bastard,' Kevin muttered as he put an arm around her shoulders and gave her a comforting hug.

She sagged sidewards against his chest wall, tears still spilling down her cheeks.

'I hate to see you like this,' Kevin grated out. 'You don't deserve it. You deserve someone to love you to death. I'm sorry that wasn't me, Michele. It was selfish and wrong of me to stay as long as I did. But I just hated hurting you.'

Blinking, Michele glanced up at him. He smiled and dropped a peck on her forehead. 'You're one special girl.'

His gentle words healed the old hurt of his betrayals, but did nothing for her present situation.

'You know, maybe we're not being fair to Tyler here. Maybe he's fallen in love for the first time in his life and he really means to be faithful. Let's face it, his asking you to marry him is pretty amazing, anyway.'

'Oh, thank you very much,' she sobbed.

'I don't mean it like that. I only meant marriage is a radical change in lifestyle for him.'

'Maybe he's doing it for the family.'

Kevin frowned. 'The one he has? Or the one he might want to have?'

'The one he has. His father wants him married.'

Kevin slowly shook his head. 'No. No, I don't see Tyler getting married on his father's say-so. Tyler's his own man. That I do know. He makes his own mistakes, and his own decisions. Look, now that I've had time to get over my initial reaction, I think you might be worrying for nothing. If Tyler says he loves you, then he does. If he's asked you to marry him, then it's because he sincerely wants to. For himself, not his father.'

Michele straightened in her chair, dabbing at her eyes with the serviette. 'Do you honestly mean that?'

'I do, indeed.'

The burst of relieved joy in her heart was so intense that she threw her arms around Kevin and kissed him.

'Hey, careful!' he protested laughingly. 'I'm a married man. Someone might see me being kissed by my ex!'

'Serves you right for stringing me along as long as you did.'

'I made you the woman you are today.'

'Which is?'

'Incredible.' And he kissed her back. 'I have to go now, Michele. My lunch-hour's over.'

'I've got the afternoon off.'

'Why don't you ring Tyler? Tell him yes to that proposal of marriage.'

'I might just do that.'

Michele smiled a soft smile as she watched Kevin walk off. He really wasn't such a bad guy. She'd forgotten how sweet he could be.

After he'd disappeared, she reached into her bag and pulled out her mobile.

'If it's Tyler you're thinking of ringing,' a cut-glass voice said from nearby. 'Then I wouldn't bother if I were you.'

CHAPTER FIFTEEN

MICHELE WHIPPED her head round to find Cleo standing there, glaring at her with killer eyes.

'I could strangle you, do you know that?' she hissed. 'Though I think Tyler might have liked to do the honours after seeing that touching little reunion between you and Kevin just now. We were up there having lunch,' she said, pointing to an upper-floor window in a nearby waterside restaurant, 'when Tyler spotted you. He was going to come down and get you when Kevin appeared. Needless to say he changed his mind at that point.'

'Where is Tyler?' A pale-faced Michele was already on her feet, searching the crowds of tourists and lunch-goers. 'I must go to him and explain!'

'He's gone. And you haven't a chance of explaining *anything* to him. When he saw you kiss Kevin that was it! My God, you should have seen his face.'

Panic and fear fizzed along Michele's veins. 'But it wasn't like that. He's got it all wrong!'

'Tell that to the tooth fairy, because Tyler won't be listening. And neither will I. I knew you didn't love him,' Cleo raged on 'and that you'd go back to Kevin if he ever asked you. I warned Tyler, but he wouldn't listen. I guess he loves you too much. And he's waited for you for too long.'

'What do you mean?' Michele gasped. 'Too long?'

'For pity's sake,' Cleo sneered, 'are you blind about every man you ever meet? Tyler's loved you for so long it's sickening. Probably since the first day he met you.'

Michele could hardly believe what she was hearing. Tyler had loved her all along? It was crazy.

And yet it made a perverse kind of sense. It also put a different complexion on everything he'd done over the years. The invitations to Kevin and herself, even when it had become obvious he no longer liked Kevin. His persistent phone calls whenever Kevin had dumped her. His taking her out to coffee whenever she was down.

Her mind raced over everything he'd said and done since Kevin's wedding invitation came, and her heart bled for him. It bled for herself, too, because his love had always been there for her but she'd never seen it.

'I...I didn't know,' she said wretchedly. 'He never said anything.'

'Why would he? You never gave him the time of day, except to argue with him. You took his friendship for granted and spent your whole time criticising him, simply because he had money. Why, I don't know! Do you think it's easy being born rich? Hell, he could have ended up a drug-addict or a spoiled, self-indulgent drop-out, like a lot of his well-off mates. Instead, he studied hard and became a success in his own right, yet all you ever did was throw his wealth and success up in his face!'

'Please don't,' Michele cried. 'I can't bear it.'

But Cleo had no pity for the girl who'd just destroyed her brother. 'Why do you think he went out with so many different girls?' she jeered. 'To try to forget you, of course. But it never worked. How could it when they weren't you? I hoped that one day he would get over you, but I knew that hadn't happened when he came to me at the beginning of this year and asked me to make over the boat-house into something less...playboyish. When I saw him with you at Kevin's wedding, I was so afraid for him.

'Then, when he brought you home the other night and you said you cared for him, I began to have a little hope. I thought you might have finally seen past the façade to the truly fine person Tyler really is.

'But it was a foolish hope,' she went on sneeringly, whilst a huge lump filled Michele's throat. 'You've broken his heart, do you know that? My God, you should have seen the look on his face when you threw your arms around Kevin and actually kissed him!'

Michele almost burst into tears on the spot. 'You don't understand,' she choked out. 'I don't love Kevin. I love Tyler.'

'Oh, come on! Do you expect me to believe that?'

'It's true, I tell you. But I've been worrying that he didn't really love me back. I thought... Oh, what does it matter what I thought now? I ran into Kevin today by accident and he asked me how things were going between Tyler and me. When I got upset and confessed my doubts about our relationship he told me not to doubt Tyler, that if Tyler said he loved me then he did. He made me see the truth for once. That's why

I kissed him. It was relief and gratitude. Nothing more.'

Cleo groaned. 'Oh, God, what a mess!'

Michele agreed. But the temptation to subside into the mangled mess was quickly replaced by a resolve to *do* something. She couldn't bear to think of Tyler thinking she didn't love him, or that she'd gone back to Kevin.

'Where do you think Tyler might have gone?' she asked.

'Not back to work, that's for sure. He'll want to be alone somewhere to lick his wounds. Tyler's very private when it comes to emotion. He hides things. Pretends there's nothing wrong. But I doubt he can pretend about this. I've never seen him so distraught.'

'I have to find him. Do you think he might have gone home? I mean…to the boat-house?'

'Possibly…'

'It's worth a try. Better than doing nothing.'

'I'll drive you. I have my car parked not far away.'

'Great. Let's go.'

Tyler's car was there, in the garage.

The boat-house door was open, but the downstairs was empty.

Michele didn't call out as she entered, nervously clutching her handbag. She hurried across the polished wooden floor and went up the steps to the loft above, knowing exactly where she would find him.

And there he was, sitting in that same armchair, staring silently into space. No coffee this time. No drink of any kind. Just silence, and a coldly implacable stare.

'Tyler?' she said huskily from across the room, and his head jerked her way.

She sucked in sharply at the haunted expression which didn't disappear swiftly enough.

'What are you doing here?' he said in the most awful voice. So flat and so defeated. 'No, don't tell me. Cleo. She never knows when to give up, that sister of mine. So what did she tell you?' he went on wearily. 'The truth about my feelings for you? I rather suspect she did, given the pitying expression in your eyes.

'So why have you come here? To face the truth at long last? To apologise? To beg my forgiveness for finding out who you really love? Because if so, then don't bother. I saw it for myself. It's still Kevin who has your heart. It will always be Kevin who has your heart. Now go away. There's no reason for you to stay. I'm not about to kill myself. Though it did briefly cross my mind when I saw you in Kevin's arms once more. I didn't think anything could hurt as much as that, but I was wrong.'

'Tyler, don't!' she cried, distressed beyond bearing by his despair. 'Please don't! You have it all wrong. You saw it all wrong.'

He made a scoffing sound as he levered himself out of the chair and onto his feet. 'I saw it all right, honey. There's nothing wrong with my eyes. Now, are you going to go under your own steam or do I have to escort you to the door?'

Her chin lifted determinedly, her fingers curling

over to grip her handbag all the tighter. 'I'm not going anywhere till you listen to me.'

His smile was wry. 'Same old Michele. You always did want the last word. So have it, sweetheart. Then go.'

Her head whirled with trying to find a place to start. In the end, she just started. 'I ran into Kevin by accident, not design. What you saw was my crying over you, not him. That's why he put his arm around me. I kissed him because he told me to stop doubting your love for me; that if you said you loved me then you did, because that was the kind of great guy you were.'

'*Kevin* said that?' Tyler looked thunderstruck.

'Yes. Then, after he was gone, Cleo tore strips off me and told me how long and how much you'd loved me.'

'Good old Cleo.'

'Yes, good old Cleo. Because it was just what I needed to hear. I love you, Tyler. I love you so much it hurts. But I did have my doubts about your loving me back, for which you only have your silly self to blame. What do you think I thought after seeing that endless parade of penthouse pets gracing your arm? I thought you were nothing but a playboy where women were concerned. But thanks to Kevin and Cleo now I don't doubt your love. And I don't think you're a playboy. I think you're wonderful. If you ask me again to marry you, I'll say yes so fast it'll make your head spin.'

If Tyler had been thunderstruck before, now he was dumbstruck for a few seconds. 'You mean that?' he managed at last. 'You really don't love Kevin any more?'

'Of course I don't, you idiot! Why do you think I'm standing here with my knees knocking? If I loved Kevin I wouldn't be here at all. I'd be too ashamed to show my face. I told you I'd never have anything more to do with him again like that, and I meant it. Not that he'd ever ask me to. He loves Danni. He told me so. And you know what? I believe him. He sounded genuinely sincere. Or as sincere as Kevin can be,' she added with a rueful laugh.

He just stared at her a while longer, before a slow smile pulled at his mouth. It pulled at her heart as well.

'You do realise that if you become my wife you'll have to be my love slave for ever.'

Her lips twitched as she tried to keep a straight face. 'A difficult job, but someone's got to do it. After all, your dad really wants you to get married and have a family of your own.'

'You want children?' He sounded surprised.

'I want yours.'

His face suddenly grew serious. 'I won't be unfaithful to you,' he said as he walked slowly towards her.

She gulped down the lump in her throat. 'I know you won't.'

'All those other girls... Some of them were only for show, you know. And the others...well, I'm only human, and they made it so damned easy for me.'

'I know...'

He stopped in front of her, his hand trembling as it

reached to gently touch her cheek. 'I never loved any of them. It's always been you, Michele. Only you...'

Her heart was so full she thought it would burst. 'I believe you.'

'Marry me,' he urged. 'Marry me and make me complete.'

Complete...

That was the right word. Complete. It said it all. For without Tyler as her husband she would only ever be half a person. And he felt the same way about her. She could see it in his eyes.

'Yes,' she agreed. 'Oh, yes.' And, dropping her handbag, she threw herself into his arms.

*Three magnificent millionaires from
Down Under—
it's high time they were married!*

Meet Tyler, Harry and Val…

The Australian Playboys

in Miranda Lee's racy, sexy new
three-part series.

THE PLAYBOY'S PROPOSITION
#2128

THE PLAYBOY'S VIRGIN
#2134

THE PLAYBOY IN PURSUIT
#2140

*Available in September, October and November in
Harlequin Presents® wherever Harlequin books are sold.*

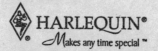

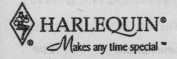

Romance is just one click away!

online book **serials**

➤ *Exclusive* to our web site, get caught up in both the daily and weekly online installments of new romance stories.

➤ Try the Writing Round Robin. Contribute a chapter to a story created by our members. Plus, winners will get prizes.

romantic **travel**

➤ Want to know where the best place to kiss in New York City is, or which restaurant in Los Angeles is the most romantic? Check out our Romantic Hot Spots for the scoop.

➤ Share your travel tips and stories with us on the romantic travel message boards.

romantic reading **library**

➤ Relax as you read our collection of Romantic Poetry.

➤ Take a peek at the Top 10 Most Romantic Lines!

Visit us online at

www.eHarlequin.com

on Women.com Networks

THE BARONS

A Texas family you can welcome into your heart

Sandra Marton's bestselling family saga
moves to the desert when Amanda,
Jonas Baron's stepdaughter, becomes...

MISTRESS OF THE SHEIKH
Harlequin Presents® #2136
On sale October 2000

Don't miss it!

Available wherever Harlequin books are sold.

Coming Next Month

HARLEQUIN *Presents*

THE BEST HAS JUST GOTTEN BETTER!

#2133 INNOCENT SINS Anne Mather
Eight years ago Laura Neill had innocently stolen into her stepbrother Oliver's room and discovered ecstasy in his arms. This is Laura's first visit home since. Can she face Oliver without confessing the love she still feels for him?

#2134 THE PLAYBOY'S VIRGIN Miranda Lee
Brilliant advertising tycoon Harry Wilde needed a challenge. It came in the guise of Tanya, who'd recently inherited an ailing firm. In no time at all Harry had helped her take charge—and had fallen for her. But Tanya wasn't the marrying kind—and he only ever had affairs....

#2135 SECRET SEDUCTION Susan Napier
Nina had lost her memory, but it was clear that stranger Ryan Flint recognized her. He seemed angry with Nina, and yet intent on seducing her. When their passion finally exploded, what secrets would be revealed?

#2136 MISTRESS OF THE SHEIKH Sandra Marton
Sheikh Nicholas al Rashid is hailed in his homeland as the Lion of the Desert, and Amanda has been commissioned to refurbish his already luxurious Manhattan apartment. Just why does Nick seem so intent on making Amanda his mistress?

#2137 A MOST PASSIONATE REVENGE Jacqueline Baird
When Rose meets society bachelor Xavier Valdespino again, he immediately whisks her to Spain and blackmails her into marriage. But despite their steamy love life, Rose soon discovers Xavier's true motivation: revenge!

#2138 THE BABY BOND Sharon Kendrick
Normally Angelica would have liked nothing better than to look after Rory's orphaned nephew—she adored babies. But this baby was her ex-husband's love child, and Rory was the brother-in-law who'd always held an illicit attraction for her....